CHAS WILLIAMSON
Paradise Series: Book Two

ECHOES
in Paradise

Print ISBN: 978-1-64649-016-5

eBook ISBN   978-1-64649-017-2

 Year of the Book

135 Glen Avenue

Glen Rock, PA 17327

Dedication

This book is dedicated to Janet, my dream girl, the love of my life, the girl who fills my heart when I'm with her and walks my dreams when we are apart. I am a man of words, yet I lack the ability to express the feelings you stir in my heart. Seeing you the first time moved me in a way I'd never felt before. And now, over fifteen thousand days later, your presence still moves me, still invigorates every cell of my being. And it thrills me to know we will be together throughout eternity, even after this life is over.

You, my love, have taught me about love, about how a man should be. Intentionally or not, you have shaped me into the man I am, the man I want to be, the man I'm proud to be. Thank you for encouraging me, believing in me and helping me fulfill my dreams.

Acknowledgments

To God, for the explosive blessings you pour out on all of us, especially me.

To Janet, my best friend and soulmate, for being there, every step of the way.

To Demi, publisher extraordinaire, for helping me grow and improve every project we undertake.

To my beta readers, Connie, Jackie, Sarah and Janet for their suggestions, help and guidance.

To Debbie Macomber, for inspiring me through your romance novels.

For authors who've inspired me through the imagery of your works. On your pages, I traveled a million miles, died a thousand deaths, shed a billion tears and dreamed of the worlds you've created. I'm honored to walk in your footsteps.

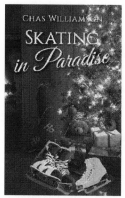

Prelude

Hannah Rutledge pulled into her driveway, trying to act as calmly as possible. Her heart raced out of control. She whipped her head from side to side and examined the street and the cars parked there. Nothing out of place. Hannah dug through her purse until she found the canister of mace. The metal can was cold in her right hand. House key in her left, she raced to the door, unlocked it and jumped inside. *Breathe normally.* Her back was against the door, as if that would keep them out.

Four-year-old Missi reached up to Hannah. "Mommy."

Her teenage daughter Beth watched her with curious eyes. "Mom? What gives? You look like you've seen a ghost. Are you okay?"

No, none of us are okay. Hannah slid the security chain across the door before hitting her knees and engulfing both daughters in her arms.

Beth tried to push her away. "Mom. Knock it off. What's going on?"

Hannah grabbed her daughter's shoulders. "Where's your phone?"

Beth tried to wriggle from her grip. "In my back pocket. Why?"

"Hand it here, now."

"What? No. Not until you tell—"

Hannah yanked the phone from her daughter's pocket and ran to the kitchen. Beth was one step behind her.

"What are you doing? Give me back my phone."

Hannah threw Beth's phone on the butcher block counter and then deposited hers next to it. *Got to destroy them.* She grabbed the meat tenderizing hammer and proceeded to pulverize both devices to smithereens.

Beth screamed, "Mother! What are you doing? That's my phone. I paid for it myself. How dare you..."

Hannah grabbed Beth's arms. "Be quiet and listen. Grab your suitcases and pack everything you can. Do *not* take your computer."

Beth's hands were on her hips. "Not until you tell me..."

Hannah pointed a finger at her daughter's face. "Don't start with me. This is an emergency. Pack and be down here in five minutes and not another word from you."

"Oh yeah? And if I refuse?"

Chills ran down Hannah's back. *I don't have time to explain.* "If you don't, you might die... or worse. Get moving, now."

Beth's face turned white. "What happened?"

Hannah was fighting back sobs. "Just do it. You've got five minutes." Hannah grabbed Missi and ran to the little girl's room. Missi was upset,

2

probably because of the heated exchange between Hannah and her eldest. Hannah yanked her daughter's Minnie Mouse roller bag from the closet and stuffed essentials inside. Her last stop was the room she used to share with her husband Dave. In three minutes, she packed what she needed, sending one last look over fifteen years of memories that filled the bedroom.

Beth appeared at the door just as Hannah zipped the suitcase shut. Her oldest had tears in her eyes and was breathing hard. "Tell me what's happening, please."

"We'll talk later. Drag these downstairs. Head to the kitchen and grab all the food you can. We can eat in the car."

"Where are we going?"

"To freedom."

"What?"

Hannah didn't mean to, but her voice came out as a scream. "Don't ask questions. Just do it, now!"

Within ten minutes, all the bags were loaded. Missi was crying and Beth tried to soothe her. Hannah's vision blurred as she backed out of the drive. *Last time we'll see this place.*

Hannah drove at the speed limit, her eyes flitting back and forth between the road and the rear view. No one was following. *Yet.* "Beth, did you bring your computer?"

"Mom, I have to have some way to talk to my friends. I need it."

"Hand that thing up here, now." Beth wasn't happy about it, but complied with her mother's request. Hannah opened the laptop, wound down the window and threw the computer onto the road. She slammed the transmission into reverse and ran over the device three times.

Beth screamed at her. "What the...? What's going on? It's got my homework and everything else on it. Why did you do that?"

The flashing lights of a police car suddenly split the night from behind them. Hannah's hands trembled as she pulled over. She grabbed the mace and snapped off the lid. *Lord, guide my hands. Help me get my girls to safety.* A sigh of relief escaped her lips when the patrol car tore past her parked vehicle.

Beth was beside herself. "Explain what's happening, now."

Hannah pulled back onto the road and pointed the car to the freeway ramp. "You'll thank me someday. I just saved your life."

Chapter 1

Five months later...

Hannah tucked the shirt into her dress pants before walking into the living room of their new apartment. Hopefully the place where they'd finally make a new start.

Beth glared at her and walked into the kitchen. Hannah followed. *Please, not another fight.*

"I'll be back in a couple of hours, after my interview."

Beth opened the refrigerator door, making sure she didn't look at her mother. "Oh what, we're staying this time?"

"Hopefully. I know you're angry with me about all this, but it was for your own good."

Her daughter whipped around to face her. Was her look anger or hatred? "Yeah, right. Saving my life again?"

"Beth, you don't understand."

Beth's eyes flashed wildly. "No. I understand perfectly. You took me away from my home. Away from my friends and you won't even tell me why. I can't get online. I can't call my friends. What the hell, Mother? You know..."

Hannah grabbed her daughter's arm. "That's enough. How dare you curse in our home?"

Beth slapped her arm away. "Home? We had a wonderful home, but you took us away in the middle of the night. All because of 'some bad people'. The only 'bad people' are the ones in your head. You're crazy and you know what? I hate you. You hear me? I hate you!"

Beth stormed down the hall and once again, Hannah followed. "Fine. Hate me, I don't care, but I need you to watch your sister while I'm gone."

"Like I have a choice. Let me tell you something. When I turn eighteen, I'm out of here and heading right back to Oklahoma."

I wish you'd trust me. "Thank goodness we have four years before that."

"Three years, four months and eleven days and you'll never see me again." Beth turned to her little sister. "Come on, Missi. Let's just watch *Little Mermaid*, and I think we'll be safe from 'bad people'."

***

Henry Campbell glanced at the clock. His interview candidate was forty minutes late. *If she shows at all.* His brother Harry was eating pork rinds, reading the *Lancaster Farmer* to pass the time. Henry flipped open the file, looking for a number to call. *Of course.* Under telephone number, she'd marked 'none'.

Henry replaced the file in the cabinet and turned to Harry. "Guess she's a no-show. I need to get back to Ellie. This close to giving birth, I don't want my wife to be alone too long."

Harry stood, stretched and scratched his head. "Sophie's with her."

Henry laughed. "My point precisely."

Before he could take another step, the door flew open. A woman with strawberry blonde hair tumbled in. Her face was red and wet, her hair matted with sweat. "I'm sorry. My car ran out of gas. Am I too late?" She was gasping for air when she extended her hand to Harry. "I'm Hannah Rutledge. Are you Henry Campbell?"

Harry shook her hand and smiled. "Nope."

Her eyebrows raised as she stared at Harry.

Henry laughed and extended his own hand. "That's my brother, Harry. I'm Henry Campbell. We'd just about given up hope on you coming."

Hannah frowned. "I'm sorry. The car's gas gauge quit working a while ago and I... I ran out of gas."

Henry motioned to a chair. "Not a problem. Make yourself comfortable and have a seat. After the interview, I'll have someone get a can of gas for you. Like something to drink?"

Her face lit up. "Please. I ran the last three miles to get here."

Harry retrieved three bottled waters from the fridge and handed one each to Hannah and Henry. The man of few words plopped down on his chair and stared at her as he gulped down his water.

Henry cleared his throat. "So Hannah, what brings you here to us?"

"I, uh, saw you had an opening, on your sign out front. I filled out an application and the woman told me to come back today. Again, I apologize for being late."

Henry hoped his smile would put her at ease. "It's fine. We're easy going here. Tell us about your work history."

"Well uh, it's been a long time since I worked outside the home. I was a waitress, about fourteen years ago."

Harry leaned toward her. "You sturdy?"

Hannah shot him a confused look. "What kind of a question is that? Am I sturdy?"

"Yeah. Lots of hard work to do."

"I'm a mother. I always work hard. Don't think that just because I'm a woman..."

Harry nodded. "Okay. You dependable?"

Hannah glanced at Henry before answering. "Of course."

Harry snickered. "Show up on time often?"

Henry bit his lips to keep his laughter inside. *My brother.*

The woman's face reddened. "I apologized about today. Usually I'm on time."

"Good. You drive?"

"Yes."

"Trucks?"

"Trucks? What kind of trucks? Pickups?"

Henry laughed. "Excuse my brother. These are his hard interview tactics."

Harry shot his brother the stink eye. "When can you start?"

"I, uh, don't even know what I'd be doing."

"Work."

"Work?"

"Yeah. Work. You know, doin' work stuff."

"Work stuff? Can you be more specific?"

Henry held his stomach as a guffaw erupted. "I'm sorry, Hannah. I've been grooming Harry on his interviewing skills, but as you can guess, it's a work in progress. This is a laborer position. You'd help harvest crops in the greenhouses and also tend our stand at local farmer's markets. Perhaps the best thing is for Harry to show you around." Henry checked his watch. *I need to get home to Ellie.* "I want to stop by the house and see my wife. We're expecting. Let's meet back here in say, an hour? If you're interested, we'll discuss the details then. Okay?"

Hannah searched both men's faces. "I-I guess."

Henry stood and shook her hand. "Forgive Harry. He's really nice once you get to know him."

Harry stood and handed her a set of keys. "You drive. I'll give directions."

"What?"

"Said you drive trucks, right?"

"I, uh, did."

"Well then. Let's go. White pickup."

Henry shook his head as the pair walked out. *I hope Harry doesn't scare this one off, too.*

***

Hannah Rutledge carried Missi on her hip. The argument with Beth continued to drag on. "You are going, young lady. No ifs, ands or buts. Get your behind into the car, now."

The girl's hands were on her hips. "And if I refuse? What else can you do to me? You moved me

9

away from my friends. You won't let me have a phone and you look over my shoulder every second I'm on the computer. We can't have an e-mail account. What else can you do, starve me? I'm almost an adult. I can't wait to leave you. Why do you always have to treat me like a baby?"

Hannah stopped to look at her daughter, standing there with her jaw clenched and her mind closed. Beth was her baby, the first one she gave life to. Hannah hated their fights, the constant bickering, and the distance between them. *I'll try a new approach.* "Okay, Beth, you win. You tell me you're almost an adult. Let's make a deal. Show me you can act like a grownup and I'll treat you as one. Clear your mind and act mature for this picnic and I'll reward you with fifteen minutes of uninterrupted computer time. I *promise* not to look over your shoulder. What do you think?" Hannah offered her hand to her daughter.

Beth appeared to be speechless. "When can I have my own cell phone?"

"Let's cross one bridge at a time. If this agreement goes well, maybe you and I can come up with a plan of rewards, increasing your freedom. Maybe, just maybe, if you show me you can act like the wonderful, grown up girl I know you are, then we can discuss getting you your own cell phone at Christmas. How does that sound?"

Hannah could see the wheels turning in Beth's mind. Beth shook her mother's hand. "We have ourselves a deal, Mother."

Hannah strapped Missi in the car seat, then turned to grasp her eldest in a hug. *I know you don't believe it, but I love you.* Beth didn't return the embrace, but at least she didn't shove her mother away like she had been doing lately.

Surprisingly, Beth broke the silence of the ride. "So, are you going to take this job?"

"I'm not quite sure yet, but I might."

"What's holding you back from taking it, Mom?"

Hannah almost swerved off the road. *She called me Mom!* This was the first time Beth had called her that since they left Oklahoma in the dark of night.

Shocked, Hannah had to compose herself. "I don't know. The money's okay and the benefits are great. Seems to be perfect, but maybe a little too perfect. It was nice of them to invite us to the company picnic today. I want to talk with some of the other employees to get their take on it. Beth, when we are there..."

"Geez, Mom. Give me a chance to show you I'm an adult. And just so you know, we'll talk about me using the private time on the computer first, so you don't think I'm browsing some perverted porn site."

That thought never crossed my mind. "Thank you, honey. I know the sudden move was hard and you miss your friends. Maybe you can chat with them on Skype, but don't tell them where we moved, okay?"

"Why's it such a big secret?"

How should I answer? She decided to try honesty, since her daughter wanted to act grown up. Hannah glanced in the rearview at Missi. The little girl was wearing a headset as she watched *Tangled* on the Blu-ray player. *Good. Don't want her to hear this.*

After checking the road, she glanced across the front seat at Beth and drew a deep breath. "Do you remember Dale?"

"Dale Olphin? Dad's friend?"

Hannah shivered at the thought of the man. "*Not* friend, coworker. That's the one. I want to try and explain something to you. Just before we moved, he tried to force me to do things with him."

Hannah wasn't sure how Beth would respond, but she knew she had to keep going now that she'd opened the door. "He wanted to use me, to control my life. When I refused, he threatened that if I wouldn't be with him, he'd make sure I'd never be with anyone else, ever."

Hannah chanced a glance at her daughter. Beth's face was white and her eyes were opened wide.

"I told him I would go to the police if he didn't leave me alone," she continued. "He laughed and reminded me his brother's the county sheriff. When he also said I had two daughters I couldn't be with every minute of every day, I panicked."

Beth covered her mouth. Her eyes were moist. Hannah swallowed hard before continuing. "You might not understand why I reacted like I did, but you and Missi are everything to me. My entire life. I moved us in the middle of the night to get as far away from him as possible. I hope he was just trying to get into my head, but when it comes to you two, I won't take any chances."

Beth was silent. Hannah again removed her eyes from the road to look at her daughter. Beth's brows were furrowed. "Mom, I didn't know. Sorry I gave you such a hard time. Why didn't you tell me before?"

Hannah had to wipe her eyes. "Because I looked at you as a child, not an adult. I realize now that was a mistake. I'm sorry, sweetheart." She lifted the turn signal switch as they reached the drive to the Campbell residence. "Looks like we're here."

***

Sam Espenshade walked into the Campbell's Celebration Barn. *Glad Harry talked me into coming.* He didn't know what was on the menu, but the enticing scent of roasted meat had his mouth watering. Sam surveyed the crowd for a place to sit. His eyes stopped on a face he recognized but hadn't seen in a while, Ashley Snyder. Sam's memories of Ashley were bittersweet. The poor girl had fought off cancer, twice. They were close friends until he graduated and moved on to play baseball. *When the world was simple, before everything changed.* His first kiss belonged to Ashley, on a Valentine's Day when he was sixteen. She'd been so frail. The chemo had robbed her of her hair, but there had always been something that attracted him. *Got to talk to her.*

Sam sneaked up behind her and covered her eyes. "Guess who?"

Ashley pulled his hands away, then jumped up and hugged him.

"Sam. What are you doing here?"

His smile had to be ear to ear. He pulled back but kept his arms around her waist. "Missed you,

Ash. I work here. You look great... and happy. You work here now, too?"

Before she could answer, Harry appeared with a plate full of food. Harry's face was bright red and his voice came out as a growl. "Get your hands off my girlfriend, right now, or I'll rip off your arm and beat you to death with it."

Sam's mouth was dry. He backed away. "Sorry, boss. I didn't know. Ashley and me, well..."

Ashley stepped between the two men. "Harry! Stop it. Sam is one of my oldest and dearest friends. He used to visit with me after I came back from chemo. Sam even shaved his head to support me when I lost my hair."

Harry's face softened as he extended his hand to Sam. "Sorry. Misunderstood. Thank you for being kind to my princess." Harry kissed Ashley's head. "Ashley's my girlfriend, my princess and my world. I apologize." Harry pulled out Ashley's chair. "Sit with us, Sam."

Sam needed a few minutes to calm down. "Thanks. I'll grab my food and be right back." His hands were still shaky when he returned.

Harry was his boss and definitely a man not to have mad at you. To Sam's surprise, there were three other people now seated at the table. There was a pretty teenage girl, a toddler and perhaps the most beautiful woman he'd ever seen. The world seemed to stop as his eyes took her in. Her strawberry blonde hair was shoulder length, and silky. Lips plump and moist. *What do they taste like?* But the most wonderful thing about her were those dark green eyes hidden behind her glasses. *Eyes of an angel.* Sam took off his ball cap and scooted closer. He couldn't peel his eyes off the woman, even when an older couple joined the table. His cheeks warmed when he realized she'd noticed him staring at her. Yet he couldn't look away.

Harry broke the spell. "Sam, I'd like to introduce you to Hannah... uh, what was the last name again?"

Her engaging smile and laughter touched Sam deep inside. It reminded him of a songbird's call.

"Rutledge. Hannah Rutledge. And these are my daughters, Beth and Missi." Hannah extended her hand toward Sam. He reached for it in anticipation, but the teenager grabbed his hand first.

"I'm Beth. And who are you?"

He answered, but couldn't take his eyes off the mother. "I'm Sam Espenshade. I work here."

Harry clapped his shoulder. "Special moment for you, Sam."

Sam could feel the warmth cover his face. *Is it that obvious?*

"Hannah's your new partner. You're now Team Echo."

His face cooled a little until he caught Hannah's grin. *She saw right through me.*

"Is it Mrs. or Miss Rutledge? Can I call you Hannah?"

The green-eyed beauty laughed. "It's *Ms.* And please call me Hannah."

"Wow, you really look good for an old woman."

Hannah's mouth dropped open. One of the older workers, an Amish lady named Mrs. Stoltzfus, hissed at him. "Samuel! Where be your manners, boy? Find them now or I'll have Jacob take you

15

behind the barn for a little talking to. He'll teach you."

Sam's eyes drifted down. *Figures. Meant it as a nice thing, but it came out wrong.* "I'm sorry, ma'am. Didn't mean no disrespect."

Hannah's eyes were laughing. "That's okay. I'll take it as a compliment. How old are you, by the way?"

"I'm twenty, almost twenty-one. How old are you?"

Again, Mrs. Stoltzfus huffed at him. "Samuel."

Hannah laughed, and again, it made his chest tingle. "It's okay. I'm not ashamed of my age. I'm thirty-two. Pleased to meet you, Samuel, or do you prefer I call you Sam?"

He fired a sidelong look at Mrs. Stoltzfus. "Call me Sam. I hate when people call me Samuel." He grew silent to prevent the risk of offending her. Then he took a seat across from Ashley.

Harry and Ashley engaged Hannah and her girls in conversation. While Beth didn't take her eyes off Sam, he couldn't quit looking at Hannah. So pretty, so sweet. But Hannah's eyes were on Harry. *She likes him.*

Before too long, Henry stopped at a nearby table, speaking with one of the older Amish men. Henry then called for everyone's attention. The Amish gentleman gave a wonderful blessing. As soon as he finished, people began eating.

As they ate, Sam and Ashley caught up on her life. While it appeared Hannah ignored him, Beth seemed to hang on his every word.

Everyone helped clean up and it was time for the fun to begin. Sam gave Harry a hand deploying the curtain to split the barn. On the far side, Henry was setting up the karaoke machine. But Sam knew about the indoor snowball fight Harry had planned. Sam had helped Harry fill the big cardboard bin, so he stayed close to his boss. As soon as Harry tipped the carton on its side, Sam stuffed dozens of the fluffy, white snowballs in his shirt. Before he had a chance to do anything, Harry flung one and nailed Sam in the face. Sam gave chase, occasionally drifting back to throw one at Ashley.

Sam refilled his shirt with the fuzzy ammunition before looking for Hannah. He caught a glimpse of her silky hair and snuck up behind her. But as he cocked his arm, Harry drilled him on the side of the head. Sam threw one sidearm that hit Harry in the back.

Music started playing from the other side of the curtain. Harry dropped his snowballs and offered his hand to Ashley. They began to dance.

Sam grabbed another snowball and turned to look for Hannah. His mouth went dry when he discovered she was standing in front of him, watching his face.

"Don't tell me you were going to hit me with that, Samuel."

Sam felt his cheeks warm. "Please call me Sam."

"Okay. As soon as you drop the snowball."

His fingers released it. The closeness to this green-eyed lady sent a shiver up his spine. While he stumbled for something funny to say, Hannah's youngest daughter tossed a snowball at him. The

17

little girl giggled. *Her name was Missi, right?* She pointed at Sam's face. "Mommy, I hit Samby."

Hannah picked up her youngest, but her eyes didn't leave his face. "That's not his name. What should Missi call you?" Hannah's smile shone brightly; her beauty made him tremble.

Sam had to concentrate hard to draw his eyes off the mother. "You can call me Samby. Yeah, I like that. And you're name's Missi, right?"

The little girl shook her head. "Nope. I'm Cinderella."

Before he could answer, the music stopped and a voice called out, "Henry, I need you."

Just like everyone else, Sam ran to the other side of the curtain. He saw a woman kneeling on the stage, holding her belly. He became aware of people murmuring around him, praying.

Sam turned at the soft touch on his shoulder. It was Hannah. She was looking at the pregnant woman on the improvised stage, but she directed her question at Sam. "Who is that?"

"That's Henry's wife, Ellie. She's pregnant."

"So I gathered."

Henry grabbed the microphone and told everyone he was taking his wife to the hospital.

Beth suddenly appeared next to Hannah. "Mom, if she has her baby, can we go see them at the hospital?"

"I don't think so, Beth. We don't know them."

Sam surprised himself when he touched Hannah's hand. Hers was warm and soft. "I do, I'll take you, uh, I mean all of you to see the baby. They're having a daughter."

Hannah turned to study Sam. "I don't know about that."

Sam's head involuntarily nodded. "I do. Henry told me it's a girl."

Hannah snickered. "I meant about going to see them."

"Sure we can. We could go Monday after work."

Her look was one of puzzlement. "And you're sure that would be okay?"

"Absolutely."

Hannah's frown wasn't encouraging. "Really?"

"Yes. You heard Harry. We're a team now. Team Echo. Trust me, Hannah."

Her irises turned a darker shade of green. "Sorry, Sam. Trust has to be earned."

Chapter 2

The cold steel of the shopping cart chilled Hannah as she walked past the fresh meat section. *Why am I here?* The basket was empty.

A voice turned her skin cold. "Well, look who's here. My favorite memory, Hannah."

She whipped around to find Dale Olphin leering at her. *How did he find me?* His eyes were focused on her chest. Why was it everywhere she went, he turned up? "What do you want?"

"I was just remembering, you know, how it was. You and me, at that party."

She zipped her fleece, but his gaze didn't move. "That was a long time ago. I'm not that girl anymore." Hannah took a small step back, glancing to see if there was someone who could help her.

He laughed. "You say that, but inside? Ain't changed none. Party girl then and ya still are. You want it. I see it in your eyes." He stepped forward and grabbed her arm. "Time for a trip down memory lane. We'll pick up where we left off." He yanked her with him through the door to the storeroom. The smell of stale beer nauseated her.

Hannah screamed as she struggled to break free. "No! Let go of me! Help! Somebody help me!"

He laughed as he squeezed both arms and shook her entire body. His mouth moved toward hers.

"Mom, wake up. You're having a nightmare."

Hannah's breath struggled to escape her lungs. *Oh my God.* Her eyes flew open. Beth was the one shaking her. "Your alarm's been ringing for fifteen minutes. Are you okay?"

Hannah grabbed Beth in a deep hug, forcing herself to calm down. "Sorry. Bad dream, that's all."

Her daughter squeezed her tightly before brushing the bangs out of her eyes. "About what?"

I can't tell you. Hannah threw the covers off and slipped out of bed. Her hands were shaking uncontrollably. "Just a stupid... it's not important. Look at the time. I'm gonna be late for work."

Beth laughed. "Make sure you look pretty. Wish it was me, spending time with that Sam Espenshade fellow."

"Thankfully it's not you. I'm not really looking forward to working with him. Don't know if he's trustworthy."

Beth giggled. "With a smile like that, how couldn't he be?"

You have a point. Still, Hannah shot her a mean look.

Her daughter just shook her head and laughed. "Okay, whatever you say, Mom."

***

Sam jumped off the deck of the box truck and grabbed the rope. He stumbled, but caught himself. *Man, that hurt.* Dust rose in a cloud as the cargo door slid closed behind him. He threw the handle to lock it in place. Sam turned to his work partner. "Now we're ready for tomorrow morning."

Hannah looked as exhausted as he felt. He'd made every effort to do the lion's share of the work, but knew she must be tired.

Hannah wiped the moisture from her brow with her arm. "What time did you say we have to leave in the morning?"

"About five-thirty. Puts us at Roots Market at six. Takes about two hours to get set up. There'll be a rush of customers by eight, rain or shine." Her skin glistened from the effort to load the truck. Even though her strawberry blonde hair was askew and her clothes dirty from their tasks, she was drop dead gorgeous. "What'd you think of your first day?"

The lady wiped her hands on her jeans. "If I ever smell cantaloupe again, it'll be too soon. How many of those bins did we fill?"

"They're called gaylords and we loaded five of them."

"Will we really sell everything we put in the truck?"

Sam's leg throbbed as he stumbled over to the cooler and grabbed two bottles of water. "Not all of it. What's left after market will be delivered to the soup kitchen." He handed her the dripping container.

Hannah sipped the cold water. "You're limping. Did you hurt your leg when you jumped off the truck?"

He looked away. "No, just an old injury."

"What happened?"

I can't tell you. The tip of his nose tingled as he forced the memory aside. "Don't want to talk about it. So... what time do you want me to pick you up tonight?"

Hannah turned to him, those green eyes now icy. "Pick me up? What's that supposed to mean? Just because we're working together doesn't mean..."

His hands instinctively shot up. "Whoa. I was talking about going to see Henry's new daughter – like we talked about during the picnic. Didn't mean to upset you."

Her cheeks blushed. "Sorry. I hate controlling people and that's what I thought you... sorry. I misinterpreted. Look, I'm not so sure it's appropriate to visit them in the hospital."

Sam pointed to the house next to the Celebration Barn. "Not at the hospital. Henry brought his girls home this morning. I'm gonna stop by later. Sure you don't want to come?"

Her eyes softened as she studied him. "You're trying hard to be my friend, aren't you?" Sam nodded. "I saw how you made sure I had the easy end of the work today. Thank you. If you think Henry wouldn't mind, let's just meet there, say about six?"

"He and Ellie are great people. They'll be glad we stopped by." Sam hesitated, but his heart forced him onward. "I was thinking about heading out for fast food afterwards. You and the girls are welcome to join me, but only if you want to. Not trying to force you or anything."

A smile graced her pretty lips. "I get it. That would be nice." Then her smile disappeared. "Sam, thanks for offering your friendship. I haven't had a friend in a long time. See you at six."

"See you then." Sam watched her walk off. So beautiful, even in dirty clothes and sweaty hair. *I want to be more than your friend, Hannah, in time.*

Chapter 3

H annah pushed back her plate. When was the last time she'd eaten this much?

Missi's face was a mess, covered with chocolate ice cream. "Can Samby take me up for more ice cream?"

Hannah shook her head. "No, honey. I think all of us had enough to eat."

Sam gave her the puppy dog eyes. "Does that mean me, too? I mean, it's not every day we come to Shady Maple Smorgasbord."

Beth gave him a strange look. "How can you eat so much, yet you're so skinny?"

"Because I'm such a hard worker. Ask your mom."

Hannah nodded. "That you are, and I know why. You always work extra hard to make it easy for me, don't you?"

A crooked smile covered Sam's face. "Don't know what you're talking about."

"Um-hmm. Keep telling yourself that. Sure, help yourself." *He's so cute when he smiles.* She hesitated. "Can you see if they have any more apple fritters, and maybe bring me the smallest one?" They were scrumptious.

He winked. "Sure you trust me?"

She was impressed he remembered their conversation about trust from the day they'd met. And he constantly picked on her about it. "Just get it, smarty."

Hannah watched him walk toward the food bar. Her chest was warm. *I'm so glad you came into my life, Sam.* Over the last couple of weeks, Sam had shown them the area, as 'tourists', or so he'd put it. Strasburg Railroad, Fulton Theater, Longwood Gardens, Kitchen Kettle, American Music Theater, Dutch Apple and Dutch Wonderland. He'd really made an effort to make their lives fun. And, in the process, Sam had won Hannah's friendship.

Beth was finishing her fruit. "Think you and Sam can take us to Hershey Park again before the summer's over, Mom?"

Hershey. She'd never forget the magical day at the amusement park. "Maybe. That was fun." Sam's actions during the visit had allowed Hannah and Beth to draw close once again. Sam had spent most of the day with Missi on the kid's rides, taking her to Zoo America and to the water park. *Missi loves him.* That allowed Hannah and her eldest to have bonding time, enjoying all the fast rides together. It felt more like they were close girlfriends now than mother and daughter. *One of my favorite days of all time.*

Missi drew her attention. "I gotta go potty, Mommy."

Before Hannah could respond, Beth stood. "Me too, Cinderella. I'll take her, Mom."

"Okay." Hannah turned her head toward the food lines, looking for Sam. He was purveying the desserts. *You've become my best friend, Sam.* Their friendship was closer than any she'd experienced in her life, including the one with her husband, God rest his soul. Sam was so nice and surprisingly respectful. It seemed he was always at her place, or taking them out. And with the work partnership, they were spending most of their waking hours together. Hannah seemed to be able to read him, well most of the time, except when she asked about his leg or his family.

A motion caught her eye. Sam was waving at her from across the giant dining room. When she focused on him, he made a funny face and turned away. *Sure loves to tease me.* The day they'd met, she knew he was attracted to her. And Hannah could tell it grew deeper every day, but he tried to hide it. Maybe she was wrong. It seemed he was waiting for something, perhaps for their closeness to grow. *Into love?* Maybe he was hoping for Hannah to feel the same way. Her inner voice whispered to her heart. *You already do, don't you?*

Hannah looked up to find Sam standing before her. "They didn't have exactly what you asked for. Instead, I brought you a gift, because I need to ask you something." He was holding something behind his back.

Here we go. He's going to tease me again. She couldn't help but smile. "And that would be?"

"This." He pulled his arm from behind his back. "Do you trust me yet?" The apple fritter she'd requested was topped with whipped cream and sprinkles.

Hannah stifled back a laugh. "Is this a bribe to get me to answer how you want?"

"Nope." He quickly placed a cherry on top. "But this is."

Hannah searched his eyes. "Okay. I trust you, maybe a little."

Sam dropped two more of the red berries on the whipped cream. "How 'bout now?"

Time to tease back. She pretended she was offended. "Do you think I'm the kind of girl who can be bribed?"

His gaze changed. "Never crossed my mind. Thank you for not being like that. One day, I think you'll trust me totally, but I want to earn that privilege, not buy it."

Hannah couldn't meet his eyes. *I hope so, too.* "I guess time will tell."

***

Jake Elliot shifted in the waiting room chair, trying to get comfortable. *My life sucks.* His head was pounding. Not even the latest issue of *Sports Illustrated* took his mind off his problems.

A nurse opened the door and surveyed the waiting room. "Mr. Elliot?"

He stood. "Here."

"Dr. Rohrer will see you now."

Jake followed her back to a treatment room and the nurse pointed to a seat. She took his temperature and frowned after getting his blood pressure. "One-sixty over ninety-five. Hmm. Is it always this high?"

"No, just under a lot of stress right now." He was silent as he watched her leave.

Within a minute, a tall dark-haired man entered. He extended his hand to Jake. "I'm Joe Rohrer. Filling in at this practice. How are you, Mr. Elliot?"

"Not so good. Can't get rid of this headache. I've had it for about two weeks. Can't hardly sleep."

Rohrer read his chart before again taking his blood pressure. "Tell me about what's going on."

Over the next five minutes, Elliot told Rohrer about his work and personal problems. "Just seems like nothing's going right in my life. The plant's closing and to top it off, my ex-wife told me she's getting remarried."

Rohrer frowned and studied the chart. "I'm sorry. I can understand why you're so stressed. I think I'll order medications for anxiety and the high blood pressure." Rohrer grew quiet, waiting for Jake to look at him. "Are you having thoughts of hurting yourself?"

You have no idea what I'm going through. Jake couldn't meet the doctor's eyes. "No."

"I'll gladly give a referral to a counselor. It helps, having someone to talk to."

Elliot shook his head. "No, thanks. Let's see if the medicine does the trick."

"Okay, but I want to see you back here in two weeks. Sound good?"

"Whatever you say. You're the doctor."

After Rohrer left, Jake walked out to the checkout, handing his chart to the woman seated at the desk. The pounding in his head made his vision blurry.

The woman's face lit up as she studied him. "Jake Elliot? Do you remember me?"

She was pretty and did look vaguely familiar, but he couldn't quite place her. "Sorry, I'm bad with names."

She extended her hand. *So soft and warm.* "I'm Daisy. Daisy Good. You used to run around with my brother, Nick."

Jake took a closer look. Her collar-length brown hair framed a gorgeous face with crystal blue eyes. Nick had an annoying little sister, with braces. He used to tease her... unmercifully. *Could this woman be the same girl?* For the first time in weeks, his cheeks raised in a smile. "Daisy. Yes, I remember you, now. It's been, what, twenty years?"

Her response was immediate. "Eighteen. I remember the last time I saw you. At Nick's graduation party. How've you been?"

His smile departed. "Life hasn't been the best." A noise behind him caught his attention. It was a lady holding a fussy baby.

Daisy didn't seem to notice. "Maybe we can catch up sometime? Perhaps a cup of coffee or tea?"

The baby started crying. "Maybe. We'll see. Really nice to see you again."

"Likewise. Bye-bye."

Jake walked toward the exit, but chanced one glance back in her direction. Daisy was watching and waved. Outside, he hesitated, momentarily considering going back in to talk with her. *Forget it. Who'd ever want you?* He headed to his old truck.

***

Hannah's feet ached. After two months, she still wasn't used to being on her feet all day. The relief crew had finally arrived to take over the stand. As she reached for her bag, she saw Sam doing something she'd witnessed twice before. He removed some bills from the money box and stuck them in his pocket. Her mouth was suddenly dry. His face paled when he noted Hannah watching him. *Oh please, no. And you wonder why I don't trust you totally.*

Sam pulled at the neck band of his shirt before addressing her. "Shift's over. Ready to head back?"

I hope you're not stealing money. "Mind if I take a quick pass through the rest of the market?"

His eyes crinkled when he smiled. "Love to. Want some company?"

He'd been so nice to her, always making her job easier. Always treating her with dignity and respect. A voice nagged at her conscience. *But he might be a thief.*

"Sure."

Sam smiled as they entered the market building. "I love this candy stand. The licorice is the best, what do you think?"

"I'm partial to peanut butter cups, myself." *How could someone as nice as him be a crook?*

After they'd bought candy, they strolled side by side. *Time to address the elephant in the room.* She took a deep breath. "Something you want to tell me about today, Sam?"

His eyes were clear when he turned to her. "About what?"

"I don't know... Like maybe why you charge certain people less than others?"

He gulped before replying. "What do you mean?"

"You sold that old lady four pounds of grapes for one dollar, not six. And gave another ten pounds of potatoes for fifty cents, not three dollars. I'm betting that wasn't the only time. That's stealing, Sam."

Sam's jaw was firm as he eyed her. She could almost feel his anger, his defensiveness. "I've never stolen from this company."

"Yeah? Then explain yourself."

"Some people need a helping hand. The grape lady is on a fixed income. And the potato woman has four little kids at home. Her husband left last year. It's hard for her to make ends meet."

Okay. *He had a point there, but still.* "Did Henry or Harry give you permission to lower the prices?"

She could sense his anger growing even stronger. *Why?*

"I thought you trusted me."

Her shoulders trembled. *I almost did.* "It's their money, not yours. And while we're at it, explain why I saw you take bills from the money box at the end of our shift."

His face turned white. "You *don't* trust me."

The scent of kettle corn drew her attention momentarily. "As I told you before, trust must be earned. What's going on?"

His cheeks changed from pale to dark red. "After all this time, you still don't trust me one bit, do you? Well let me tell you something, *Ms.* Rutledge. You are not my boss and it's none of your business." Sam shook his head as he stared at her. He reached into his pocket and produced a set of keys. Sam held them in front of him. "Here."

"Why are you handing those to me?"

"Since you don't trust me, you don't have to ride with me."

"Stop it. Act like a grown up. Of course I'll ride with you."

His lips were set in a fine white line. "A grown up? Fine." He dropped them on the floor. "I don't want you to have to put up with my immaturity." Sam turned away.

Wait! "Sam, come back here. Let's talk about this like adults."

He continued to walk away. "I'm just a kid in your eyes... and an untrustworthy one at that. Don't worry 'bout me. I'll find my own way home." He disappeared into the crowd.

Of all the childish... Hannah retrieved the keys and tried to follow after him. She searched the crowd for Sam, but he'd disappeared like a wisp of smoke. *We need to talk about this.* She looked everywhere, but he was gone. Hannah found the company truck and climbed in. *Why couldn't you just be honest with me?* She really cared for Sam and wanted to trust him, but what he was doing was wrong. The thought gnawed at her while she drove home. *What should I do?* There was only one thing her conscience would allow.

After parking the truck, she walked to the office. Harry and Henry were both looking at something on the computer when she entered.

Harry nodded. "Hannah."

She didn't answer right away and waited until she caught both sets of eyes.

It was Henry who addressed her. "Hannah, are you okay?"

God, please let me be wrong about this. "Can I speak with both of you?"

Harry pulled out a chair for her. "Always. What about?"

Hannah drew a deep breath. "Sam."

Chapter 4

The nurse ushered Jake into the office and took his vitals. "Your blood pressure's high again, but it's improving. Still have the headaches?"

He nodded. "Yeah, they're pretty bad."

"Dr. Rohrer will be in shortly."

This was visit number four. The good doctor had Jake coming in weekly. He hated the thought of it, but the highlight of those visits was seeing Daisy. *Daisy, beautiful Daisy.* Her face broke into a big smile every time she saw him. Like a breath of fresh air. Daisy always asked him about getting together to catch up, but he'd said no—so far.

The door swung open and Dr. Rohrer entered. "Hey, Jake. The nurse tells me the headaches are still persisting. What's going on?"

One thing Jake liked about this doctor was his easy-going style. The visits had become more of a therapy session than a true medical visit. "My nerves are about shot." Once again, he talked about his struggles while Dr. Rohrer listened.

After Jake finished, the doctor sighed. "I'd like to believe it's only stress, but I'm going to order a head CT. That way we can rule out any physical causes. I could order prescription painkillers, but I'm reluctant to do so at this point."

Because of the opioid epidemic. It had been on the news how people were seeking them as a way to get high. *Not me.* "I understand. Not looking for those kind of drugs. Anything else you could suggest?"

"Besides the maximum dose of ibuprofen or naproxen sodium? How about a hobby or physical activity? Good ways to relieve stress. And there's the other option we've discussed. Talking to a therapist."

No way. Jake shook his head. "Don't want a shrink."

"Okay, do you have a friend you can confide in?"

"There's no one."

"Hmm, maybe you're overlooking someone." Jake was confused by the doctor's grin. "Think about it. Come back next week and we'll see how it's going. Bye, Jake."

Now that the visit was over, the best part remained—stopping by to see Daisy. But when Jake reached the checkout, a different girl was there. He cleared his throat. "Where's Daisy?"

The young woman's smirk caught him off guard. He caught the wink she gave a co-worker. "Daisy's at lunch. She'll be back in about fifteen minutes if you want to wait. Or should I just tell her you asked about her?" The girl had a know-it-all smile.

"Uh, no. That's not necessary. I'll catch her next time." He made a quick getaway to the safety of his Ford. *That was a wasted appointment.* As he was fumbling for his keys, a white sedan pulled into the next row, three spots down. He recognized the driver. *Daisy.* Despite the frown on her face, she was so pretty, like a ray of sunshine on a rainy day. The girl carried a plastic bag from a convenience store.

The clicking of her heels split the afternoon silence. *Someone to talk to...* Jake wound his window down and yelled to her. "Hi, Daisy."

She turned, eyebrows furrowed as she sought the source. Jake's heart almost stopped when her eyes found his. Her features softened. Those pearly white teeth made an appearance and she walked to his car. Somehow her hand ended up over his. *Such warmth.* A pleasant fragrance wrapped itself around him. *Hyacinths.* Daisy's scent. Her blue eyes were smiling, just like her lips. "Jake. I saw you were on the schedule, but I thought I missed you. Had an offsite meeting."

He was almost at a loss for words. *Talk to her, dummy.* "Thought I'd missed you, too. Guess our timing was good after all, huh?"

Her laughter reminded him of a waterfall. "Guess it was." She grew silent, watching his eyes.

Ask her, idiot. "I, uh, thought about what you'd, umm... suggested."

Somehow her smile widened even further. "About catching up?"

Yes! Jake's mouth was dry and his hands were suddenly sweaty. "Yeah, that's what... I mean, yes. Would you like to, maybe, uh, get a cup of coffee on Saturday?"

Daisy's smile lessened, but was still the best thing he'd seen in a while. "I work until noon and promised Mom we'd go shopping in the afternoon. How 'bout Sunday?"

Yes. He nodded rapidly. "Okay. What time and where?"

She giggled at him. "Say noon?" Jake nodded again. "I still live at home. Pick me up there? Mom and Dad would love to see you."

"Great. Would you like to do lunch?"

Daisy squeezed his hand. "I've got something better in mind—afternoon tea. Maybe afterwards, we can go for a walk, okay?"

"Sounds great."

"All righty, see you then. Bye." She started to walk away before turning. "And Jake? Thanks. Can't wait to catch up. Ta-ta."

Jake was mesmerized as he watched her walk to the door. His heart was beating so fast. Just before she entered, she turned and waved. He nodded and then started the truck. That's when it dawned on him. For the first time in weeks, his headache was gone.

***

Hannah lugged the heavy box of celery to the truck. *I'll never eat a stalk of celery again.* Some of the celery was bad and the smell all but turned her stomach. Her new work partner, Kyle Parker, was a slacker. The way the man stared at her sent eerie feelings up her spine. She finally realized how much Sam had been doing to help her. *I really screwed up.* Her mind drifted back to the conversation with the Campbell brothers. The one about Sam.

Henry had studied her face. *"What about Sam?"*

"I, oh, I hate to tell you this."

Harry sat there, arms crossed. *"Spit it out. Did he say something bad, or worse?"*

"No, it's, uh, I think... I think he's stealing from you."

Harry's chair flew backwards as he stood. She could see the veins in his temples bulge. *"What?"*

She'd closed her eyes for strength. *"I've seen him take money from the cash box at the end of our shift."*

She'd grown puzzled when the brothers shared a glance and laughed. Henry answered. *"Not the first time we've heard that."*

"What?"

Harry had nodded. *"Sam's charity."*

"I don't understand."

Henry patted her hand. *"Watch him next time, when you start up. He puts forty dollars in the cash box. He undercharges certain customers and keeps track of it. You just saw him get his change out. It's his way of helping people. Been doing that since he started."*

"Are you serious?"

"Absolutely. He asked us about it before he began. We gave permission."

Harry chimed in. *"I trust Sam like a brother. Well, at least as much as I trust Henry."*

Hannah felt like a heel of bread after she walked out. But what hurt the most was when Sam didn't show up for the next shift. It felt like she'd lost her best friend. Then Kyle appeared, announcing he was her new work partner. At the end of the day, Hannah sought out Sam. His eyes were icy.

"Sam, they told me you asked to be reassigned. Can you tell me why?"

"Gotta trust your partner. You obviously don't."

"Look, I made a mistake. I shouldn't have gone to Henry and Harry, but when I tried to talk it out, you didn't want to."

She'd never forget the look on his face, the hurt in his eyes. *"You ratted me out? To the boss?"*

"You didn't give me a choice. If you'd have simply..."

Sam's temper exploded. *"I didn't realize you thought so little of me! And to think..."* He'd wiped his cheeks as he turned.

"Why didn't you just tell me what you were doing?"

He'd whipped around to face her. *"I don't have to tell you crap. You know, I went out of my way to be nice to you. To make your life easy. To be your friend... and this is the thanks I get? I'm glad I asked for another partner."*

"Look, I'm sorry. Let me make it up to you. I bought tickets to the ball game tonight. The Barnstormers are hosting the York Revolution. I'll even buy you dinner."

His expression changed. Had it been fear or hatred? *"I HATE baseball."*

"Okay. Just come over so we can talk about what happened. It was just..." She hadn't finished because he'd stormed away. On the rare occasions she'd seen him since, he'd made sure he had some reason to get away from her, quickly.

"I hurt him. Help me make it right, God." *Friends like Sam don't come along every day.*

The overwhelming scent of Old Spice filled her lungs. Kyle. "Think I'll take a little break, girl. It's been a long day and I'm tired. Give you a hand when I get back." He headed off to the office, where the air conditioning would be blasting.

Hannah muttered under her breath, "Lazy jerk. Won't be back until the truck's full." Off in the distance, she caught sight of one of the green and yellow tractors. Sam was driving, pulling a wagon load of pumpkins. His new work partner was a young Mennonite girl named Sara. Sara was sitting on the fender, laughing. Even from a distance, Hannah could pick up the joy in the other girl's face. A chill rolled across her shoulders. *Why should it bother me?*

Sam stopped the tractor and backed the wagon to the dock. As he stood to dismount, his eyes gravitated to Hannah. Her heartbeat quickened. *I miss you, Sam. Come talk to me.* But he looked down, shook his head and then jumped to the ground. Sara held her hands out for Sam to help her, but he ignored the girl. After he disappeared into the barn, a void filled her chest. Hannah shook it off and grabbed another box to load. Why should she care? Something within her answered. *You know why.*

Chapter 5

D aisy checked the mirror one last time. *I look good.* And she did. Every strand of hair was in place. Her eye shadow accentuated the crystal blue of her irises. The cherry lip gloss glistened in the reflection.

A voice caught her attention. "You look wonderful, Daisy." Her mother, Vivian. Not just her mom, but also her closest friend. And Vivian knew the significance of the day. Daisy had waited years for this opportunity. "Where's he taking you?"

Daisy squeezed her mother's hands. "Tuscany."

"The Tea Room?"

Daisy dabbed a little perfume on her neck, not much, just enough to be subtle. "Yes. We talked about a walk afterwards. I was thinking the rail trail from Elizabethtown to Mount Gretna."

Mother eyed her heels. "Not in those shoes."

A giggle escaped from Daisy's throat. "Of course not. I'm bringing sneakers."

Her mom turned. "I'll pack a couple bottles of water for you."

"Already done, as well as some snacks."

Vivian turned and studied her daughter. "Is there anything I can do to help?"

Daisy reached for her mom's hands. "Yes. Say a little prayer for me."

She could easily see the love in Vivian's eyes. "I do, every single day."

***

Jake pulled up in front of the strange looking building. The enchanting fragrance of hyacinths filled the truck—Daisy's scent. Her smile was so beautiful. *Did I die and go to heaven?* Jake couldn't help but gaze at her.

Daisy laughed. "Were we planning on going in, or just sitting in the truck?"

Crap! He'd been too mesmerized to think about getting out. "Sorry, yes." He jumped out and raced around to hold the door for her. After she exited, he hit the lock and closed the truck door. Together, they walked to the entrance. The tinkle of a bell caught his attention.

A short, beautiful blonde met them. She had a British accent. "Welcome to Essence of Tuscany. I'm Sophie Miller. Do you have reservations?" Sophie smiled when she glanced toward Daisy. "I know you... Daisy, right? Your mother brought you here before, didn't she?"

Jake noted the easy-going smile Daisy returned. "Good memory, Sophie. Yes, and this is my very good friend, Jake."

Very good friend? *I like the sound of that.* Jake followed the two women and held the chair for Daisy. They ordered hot tea before Sophie walked away. Orange jasmine for Daisy, Earl Gray for himself. Then after their drinks arrived, they placed their food order.

"So, come here often?"

Daisy selected two cubes of brown sugar and dropped them in her cup. "Second time. I love this place. Just opened, you know?"

He took in the elegant decorations. "Quite pretty. Takes you away from the daily grind of things."

When he turned his gaze toward her, she was smiling, watching him. "Being here makes me feel like I'm in old England, at a quaint little tea house."

"Cool. Ever been there? I mean England?"

"Not yet. Maybe someday." She bit her lip and studied her cup.

She's gorgeous. Daisy took a deep breath and engaged his eyes.

"So Jake, how's life?"

He sighed. "Life didn't turn out like I hoped." Before he realized it, he told her all about his problems. How his ex-wife Callie unexpectedly filed for divorce. "Never saw it coming. I thought we were happy. To top it off, she texted me she's getting remarried, to some old guy she met online." He moved onto the issue at his job. "I've never worked anywhere else. Put my heart and soul into that factory, then out of the blue, they announced another company bought it. Two weeks later, the new owners notified everyone we were closing."

Daisy placed her hand over his. The warmth and softness of her touch moved him. "I can only imagine how hard that is. So what's next?"

Jake wiped his face with his free hand. "Not a clue. I'm the last one left. There to get rid of everything all of us worked so hard to build. In about a month, I'll be unemployed."

Daisy's voice was soft. "Don't lose faith. Everything happens for a reason. When God closes one door, He opens another." She hesitated briefly until she caught his gaze. "Many times, what's next is better than what had been."

He studied the depth of those blue eyes. Like they went on forever. Her words slowly sank into his mind. *Is she talking about work or... something else?*

Before he could respond, another girl appeared. Long, thick blonde hair. Petite, but she carried an aura of happiness with her. "Hi guys, I'm Ashley. Here's your order." Ashley went on to describe the appetizing three-tiered tray of food. "I'll bring you each another pot of tea."

As they ate, Jake couldn't stop looking at Daisy. So pretty, with an air of poise and self-confidence. Seemed like yesterday, she'd been an annoying, overweight kid with braces. *Is this really the same girl?* The Daisy of old had been obnoxious, loud and a general pain. Of course, in those days, Jake had gone out of his way to be nasty to her.

"I'm surprised you haven't asked about me. Not interested?"

His egg and onion sandwich seemed to stick in his throat. "Sorry. Didn't mean to be rude. Yes, I'd love to hear all about you. How'd you end up being a clerk in a doctor's office?"

She giggled as she shook her head. "I'm not a clerk. I'm the practice manager. I only happened to be filling in at the window the first day you came." Her cheeks seemed to redden. "After that, I just tried to be there when you checked out." Okay, her cheeks were blood red now.

She's blushing? He touched her hand. "Why's that?"

Daisy looked away. "I wanted to talk to you, that's all. Out of all of Nick's friends, you were the nicest to me."

Guilt made an appearance. He and Nick used to come up with schemes to terrorize her. To make fun of her. *I treated you like you were nothing.* "I'm sorry. Don't remember being kind to you."

A smile broke out. "I do. You were at my thirteenth birthday party. You slow danced with me that day. Remember?"

I only did that to embarrass you, to make fun of you in front of everyone. "Yes. Thanks for remembering me so kindly. I don't deserve that."

She sighed and her eyes widened for a second. She was studying the desserts, specifically the cream-filled swan pastry. "Mind if we split this one?"

"No. Help yourself. You go to college?"

Daisy bit her lip and winced before answering. "Don't remember, do you?"

"What?"

"At Millersville. You were a non-trad student. We had a technical writing class together. Remember?"

Try as he might, he didn't recollect Daisy being in the class. "No, sorry. Why didn't you say something?"

She wasn't looking at him. It was as if a cloud darkened the room. "I looked different in those days. I'd put on a lot of weight in high school. Weighed over three hundred pounds. I didn't much like myself."

"Daisy, I'm sorry."

"That's okay. That class was the turning point in my life—you not recognizing me. I vowed to change. It took me five years, but I lost all that flab. Love the way I look now." She swept her short hair back and flashed a smile at him. The clouds dissipated and the sunshine of her face now lit the room.

Me, too. "Never would have guessed that. You really look terrific." Before he asked, he prayed she would say 'no'. "So, is there a man in your life?"

Daisy's eyes left his as she concentrated on the swan. Curiosity filled his mind as she cut the pastry into small pieces. Her hands seemed to be shaking. "No. I've been waiting all these years for Mr. Right."

"And let me guess, he hasn't come along... yet."

Her eyes locked on his. "Actually, he did. But the timing wasn't quite right. I'm hoping that will change soon... the timing, I mean."

Jake's eyes could no longer meet hers. *Of all the rotten luck. I overlooked a diamond.* "It will happen, I'm sure."

"Yeah. Me, too."

They finished their meal in silence. To his surprise, Daisy grabbed the check. "Why'd you do that? I wanted to treat you."

She laughed and in his mind, he could see them at the shore. Walking hand in hand...

"You can treat next time."

"I would love that. This has been fun. Maybe we can do it again soon. I like this place." *But not as much as the company.*

Daisy's face clouded. "Aren't we going for a walk? I packed my sneakers."

Dummy! "Yes, yes. Sorry." They walked to his Ford. He reached for the carabiner on his belt loop where he kept his keys, but they weren't there. He searched his jeans. Nothing. Glancing in the window, he saw them. There on the seat. He'd been in such a hurry to get the door for her that he'd forgotten to take them. "Dang it. I locked my keys in the car."

Her laughter caught his attention. "Freudian slip? Liked this place so much, you wanted to stay for a while, huh? Or..." she hesitated briefly and her eyes seemed to grow larger, "...do you just like being with me?"

Chapter 6

Sam knelt alone in the darkening gloom. He traced the name on the granite marker. Today was her birthday. His cell vibrated in his pocket. *Riley*. Sam wiped his eyes and took a deep breath before answering. "Hey, sis."

"Hi, Scooter. Whatcha doing?"

"Nothing." Against his will, a sob escaped his lips.

Her voice grew soft. "You're there, with Jenna, aren't you?"

He palmed his eyes. "No."

"Liar. Put the phone on speaker."

Sam did, touching the letters carved in the stone.

Riley started to sing the Happy Birthday song for their dead sister. Sam tried to join in, but his words were choppy. Riley finished. "Jenna, we love you. We *will* see you again and someday, the three of us will once more be together, in Heaven."

The essence of the lilies he placed on Jenna's grave filled his mind. Sam sniffed hard. "Allergies, you know?"

"I see."

"Thanks, Riley."

"How've you been?"

The clip clop of a buggy momentarily drew his attention. "Oh, fair to middlin'."

"And Hannah? What's she doing?"

Sam ran his sleeve over his face. "Don't know, don't care."

"Right. Don't lie to me. You really care for her."

He winced. *Care for her? I love her.* "Whatever."

"Stop it. You do realize you were the one who was wrong, don't you?"

Like you'd understand. "Riley, she ratted me out. I wasn't stealing."

Riley sighed. Her voice was quieter. "You know that. I do, too. Poor Hannah didn't. Think about it. If the roles were reversed, I would have done the same thing she did."

"But she..."

"Sam, what did Mom and Dad teach us? To turn the other cheek. To walk a mile in the other person's shoes. To forgive..."

He shook his head. "But Riley..."

"...to forgive. Seventy times seven. Patch it up with her. If not for her sake, for yours."

"It's no use. She sees me as a kid."

"Then show her you're mature. Act like a man."

His eyes gravitated to his grandfather's gravestone. *Pops was a real man. I'll never measure up to him.* "I don't know how. What can I do?"

The voice on the other end of the line was momentarily silent. "Hmm, I have an idea..."

***

Hannah grabbed the trash bag and headed for the door. The odor from last evening's salmon permeated through the plastic. Missi, Beth and her new best friend, Selena, were playing with Beth's new kitten. Allowing the girls to get a cat brought some normality to the apartment. Beth had even begun referring to the flat as home. Hannah lugged the refuse to the dumpster. A horn blast from a diesel rig erupted behind her. She waved at the driver and waited for him to park. The man dismounted, threw away his cigarette and walked to her.

"Whew. Glad that week's finally in."

It was John, Selena's dad. "Where was this run?" she asked.

"Dallas. Thanks for letting Selena stay with you."

"No problem. I called out for pizza. Want to join us?"

John pulled out his wallet. The one connected to his belt loop with a heavy chain. "Only if I can pay."

"Agreed. Come on in."

John walked toward his daughter and wrapped his arms around Selena. "Come give Daddy some sugar, baby girl."

Selena tried to wriggle free. "Father! I am fifteen years old…"

John snuggled her in his arms. "And you'll always be my baby."

Selena finally pulled away, running into the living room with Beth and Missi close behind.

Something pulled at Hannah's heart strings. "They grow up way too fast, don't they?"

John sighed deeply. "Yeah. Hard raising her alone. Didn't have no choice. Her mom died when she was a toddler."

Hannah touched his arm. The odor of cigarette smoke seemed to suddenly fill the room. "What happened?"

"She died in Iraq. Roadside bomb."

"Sorry, John."

He slicked back his hair with his hand. "Not going there. Selena said you lost your husband a while back, too."

Hannah's words stuck in her throat. "He's been gone twenty months. Died in an accident at work." She looked away and grew silent.

"Well, maybe we can help each other, you know?" He shot her a wink. "We're friends, now."

Dream on. That *will never happen.* "Time will tell. Trust has to be earned, John. Sorry about that."

John studied her face. She could sense his disappointment.

"Gonna walk next door and grab a beer. Want one?"

An unpleasant memory reared its ugly head. *A single beer started the nightmare, years ago.* "John, I don't allow drinking around my girls."

John chewed his cheek. The stale cigarette scent increased. "'Kay. I'll have a slice of pizza, then head over. Send Selena home when you get tired of her." Without asking, he walked into the living room and turned a ball game on the TV.

Hannah's thoughts drifted to Sam. Since her husband's death, she'd only had one real friend. That had been Sam. *Screwed that up.* Something told her to talk to him. To patch it up. Loud music poured in through the open window. The pizza driver had arrived. But before she walked to the door, she closed her eyes. Sam's smile filled her mind. Hannah shook off the thought. *Do you even care, Sam?*

Chapter 7

J ake closed his eyes and drew deep, slow breaths to calm himself while the nurse took his blood pressure.

She studied the electronic display. "One-ten over sixty. Excellent. How are you feeling? Any more headaches?"

It was Jake's turn to smile. "This is the best I've felt in years. My headaches are gone."

Her sly smile drew his attention. "Hmm, wonder what made the difference? Dr. Rohrer will be in shortly." She closed the door behind her.

Daisy. She'd made the difference. He'd seen her every day since the initial get together at the Tea Room. Most nights they took a long walk, either down a country road to this quaint covered bridge south of Paradise or else up the North Reading Road, just below Brownstown, along the banks of the Cocalico Creek. It felt so natural, her sitting next to him as they watched the stars appear. But one thing bothered Jake. His mind drifted back to their last conversation about Mr. Right.

"We always talk about my life and problems. How's it going with Mr. Right?"

Her blue eyes seemed to glow in the dusk. *"It's never been better. Mr. Right and I grow closer every day."*

"Have you told him he's Mr. Right, yet?"

Daisy giggled. *"Not just yet, but soon."*

Jake's vision grew blurry for a few seconds. *"Does he feel the same way as you do?"*

Her smile was so lovely. *"I'm pretty sure he does, but I want to take it slow. I'm kind of waiting for him to realize he's in love with me."*

Jake shook his head as his thoughts returned to the present. "How can that be? She spends all of her free time with me," he mumbled. *Must be someone here at work.*

The door swung open and Rohrer entered with a smile. "Jake. So I hear my patient is progressing nicely. So glad you found someone to confide in."

What? "What do you mean? I didn't tell the nurse that."

Dr. Rohrer laughed. "Daisy told me. It's not a HIPAA thing. She casually mentioned the long talks. Daisy is such a nice girl. I consider her to be one of my closest friends."

Jake's mouth went dry. *Is Dr. Rohrer the secret Mr. Right?* Jake had been hoping Daisy's eyes would be open as to how Jake felt about her. *Can't compete with a man like him.* Rohrer was young, good looking, well built and a doctor to boot, if a girl was into that sort of thing. *Nothing like me.*

Jake was subdued for the rest of the appointment. His mind was elsewhere, not in the examination room. His thoughts dissipated when the doctor stood.

"Well, I think I'm going to release you from care. Seems like your blood pressure is down and your headaches are gone. Just call and schedule an appointment if you need me." Rohrer turned and left Jake sitting in the chair. His hands trembled. Jake composed himself before he went out to see Daisy. *I need to tell her how I feel. Today.*

But it wasn't Daisy sitting at the desk. It was another girl. Oh, he caught the way she motioned and smiled at the other office staff. His arms quaked. *Such a fool. I'm the butt of their joke.* Why hadn't he seen this?

He needed to see Daisy, now. "Pardon me, but could I speak to Ms. Good?"

A sound behind him drew his attention, a male voice. "Hi, Mr. Elliot. Daisy's behind closed doors with her boss." The look of confusion on Jake's face must have been evident. The man stuck out his hand, which Jake shook. "I'm Trenton, the Clinical Nurse Coordinator. Daisy and I are *very* close friends. She thought you might ask to see her, but Daisy knew she wouldn't be available." He produced an envelope from his scrub top. "Asked me to give this note to you."

"Thanks," But when Jake grasped the paper, Trenton didn't release it.

The man's eyes challenged Jake. "Be careful with her. Daisy's my girl and I don't want to see her hurt." He finally released his grip and walked off.

So Trenton is Mr. Right? He watched the red-bearded man walk off with confidence in his step. Jake's vision was wavy as he headed outside. His breathing was shallow when he climbed into his truck. Jake tore open the covering.

'Dearest Jake, I'm sorry, but I can't see you tonight. Something came up. Forgot to tell you, but I have to travel to Pittsburgh for an in-service and won't be back until Thursday. You can call me, but only if you want to. See you then. Love, Daisy.'

Jake crumpled the paper and threw it on the floorboard. His headache was back, with a vengeance.

***

Hannah bolted upright in bed, the nightmare still gripping her mind. She tried to force it away, but the haunting image of Dale Olphin flashed before her. He'd been waiting for her in the grocery store, again.

"Well, look what the dogs drug in. Hot little Hannah Murphy."

She'd tried to walk away from him, but he blocked her escape. *"My last name is Rutledge. I quit being Hannah Murphy years ago."*

Dale's laugh was sinister. *"Nope. Hannah Murphy, the life of the party. How about you and me..."* He grabbed her arm.

"Let me go. Help! Leave me alone."

He covered her mouth with his hand and forced her against the wall. *"No sense fighting it. Didn't in the old days."*

She sank her teeth into his hand. He yanked it away. Hannah slapped him. *"Get away from me."*

He laughed at her. *"You don't want to play nice? Fine. Bet it's in the blood line. Maybe your daughter will take your place."*

She kicked his leg and shoved him aside, bolting to freedom. *"I'm calling the police."*

Dale's voice mocked her. *"Go ahead. My brother's the County Sheriff. Used to party with him, too. He knows how to track your phone, your computer. You can run, Hannah, but you can't hide. You'll give us what we want, just like the old days."*

The alarm on her phone sounded. Hannah silenced it and willed herself into the shower. She made breakfast for her girls and dropped Missi off at the sitter. *I destroyed our phones, Beth's computer.* No logical way for them to track her.

The nightmare still lingered in the shadows of her thoughts as she punched in at work. She turned to find a man right behind her. Startled, she placed her hand over her mouth.

Sam Espenshade stood before her. "Morning, Hannah." He extended his hand, which held a cup from a convenience store.

"Wh-what's this?"

He frowned. "Peace offering. You were right. I did act like a child. I wanna... uh, I mean..." Sam gulped and pursed his lips. "I'm hoping you have it in you to allow me to apologize. I'd really like to talk to you, maybe after work?"

Hannah's heart fluttered. "I, uh, I don't know." *I really missed your friendship, Sam.*

His crooked smile was the best thing she'd seen in a while. "If it's not too forward, I'll take that as a yes. See you after work." Sam tipped his hat and strolled off.

Hannah walked into the greenhouse. The unexpectedly happy encounter with Sam superseded the bad dream. The taste of chocolate warmed her as she sipped the hot drink. *He remembered!*

Hannah had a hard time focusing. She polished off the mocha and dropped the empty drink container in the trash. Today, she and Kyle would be harvesting green beans. Several three-hundred-foot rows awaited them—well, her. As usual, Kyle was nowhere to be seen. He usually found his work area half an hour after the start of the shift. *Jerk.* Hannah grabbed a basket and reached for the first pod.

The hothouse door flew open and Sara, Sam's work partner, rushed in. "Hannah, come quickly. Sophie Miller's cows got out. We need help getting them back in the barnyard."

Hannah followed her outside. *This job is seldom boring.* It was easy to see Sophie's Angus bovines were wreaking havoc on the meticulously landscaped flower beds.

Sam appeared and called out. "Okay, everybody. Form a line, hands out. We'll work our way toward the barnyard. Nice and slow so we don't spook 'em. Watch that big one. He's a bull and he's mean as can be."

Hannah joined the line as they herded the cows to the barnyard. All but one were inside the fencing when the large one balked. Sam yelled, "Git in there, you good for nothin', ornery bull."

The big black mass suddenly turned and charged. Right at Hannah. She tried to move out of the way, but he butted Hannah with his head, sending her flying straight up in the air. Then the mean-spirited animal kicked his heels, striking Hannah's left leg. The force was enough to send her body pinwheeling into a lamp post. Stars immediately appeared when her head slammed into the steel pole. Everything was spinning as she tried to catch her breath. The last thing she saw before the world turned black was Sam's face, contorted in fear.

Chapter 8

J ake Elliot slipped his computer and access badge in the carton. He bit his lips to hide his feelings. "This is the last of it." He sealed the carton and handed it to the UPS driver.

The man extended his hand. "Been nice working with you. Best wishes, my friend."

Jake watched the truck pull away, and then locked the dock door. It was all he could do to hold it together as he walked through the empty building. Memories came flooding back, of the friends he'd known, the good times they'd enjoyed. "Can't believe it's over." Just like that, the new owners had closed a once successful business, moving everything overseas for foreign hands to make the product that had been built right here... in Lancaster County, Pennsylvania, USA.

The front door was heavy as he swung it open. The real estate manager was waiting impatiently. Jake handed him the keys without a word. *It's over*. He turned so the man couldn't see his emotions, taking one last look where he'd spent the last eighteen years of his life. Slowly, he shuffled across the brick walkway he'd designed and installed last year. His head was down as he approached his old Ford.

"Hey there. Thought you might need a friend today."

Daisy? The dazzling brilliance of those blue eyes was almost blinding. "What are you doing here?"

She met him halfway and wrapped her warm arms around him. The scent of hyacinths engulfed him. Her voice was barely above a whisper. "Knew you'd need me. Shouldn't be alone at a time like this."

It took a few minutes before he was able to speak. "I didn't expect to see you again."

Daisy quickly pulled away. In her eyes, he could see concern. "What in the world made you think that?"

Jake sniffed. "Trenton made it pretty clear."

"Made *what* clear?"

"That you belong to him. Told me you were his girl."

Daisy's eyes softened. "Oh, Jake. Trenton is just a good friend. I can guarantee I'm not his girl."

A buzzing filled his right ear. He waved his hand to chase away the bumble bee. "Really?"

"Trenton's gay."

Jake's mouth fell open. "What? Then why'd he say you were his girl?"

She held his hands. "I think he just meant we're close, like close girlfriends." Daisy frowned as she studied his face. "He's a complicated guy. And *just* a friend."

Jake was surprised at his words. "I thought he might be Mr. Right."

Daisy raised her eyebrows and laughed. "You did, huh?" Jake nodded. "Not even close."

"So, will I get a chance to meet him? I mean Mr. Right?"

The girl was silent as her gaze flitted back and forth between his eyes. "You already have, but I'll introduce you again when the time is right." Daisy shook her head. "Can I change the subject?"

Has to be Rohrer then. "Of course. I'm sorry."

"No worries. I came here to help you heal."

The blue in her eyes was subdued. "Help me heal?"

"Yes. I'm taking you away. Part of the healing process is mourning. I want you to tell me all about what was your job. Then tomorrow, we'll forget about everything and just enjoy our friendship. Starting Monday, we'll talk about your future."

He'd almost forgotten he'd just lost his job. "Really think I have one?"

The iridescence of those gorgeous blue eyes now shone brightly. "Yes. God may have closed this door. But He has something special planned for you. Jake, I'm going to help you find it."

***

A horrible, pungent odor made Hannah's eyes water. "What the...? Leave me alone."

"Hannah, talk to me. Are you hurt?" It was Sam, kneeling to her right. Harry Campbell squatted down to her left and threw something away. "Hannah?"

A warmth engulfed her right hand. Hannah glanced down, realizing Sam held it, tightly. "My head, it hurts."

Harry spoke. "Need to get her to the hospital. I'll drive."

Sam stood. His voice was very loud. "No. I want to take her."

Harry swept Hannah in his arms. "Okay. Take my truck."

The world was spinning again. Things were happening so fast, Hannah couldn't quite comprehend the activity. The whirling slowed. Glancing at the man in the driver's seat, she realized it was Sam. A warmth comforted her when he reached over to grasp her hand. Hannah's eyes fluttered and the fog returned, fading to black.

A voice called her name. A woman's voice. "Ms. Rutledge? Can you tell me what day it is?"

"I, uh, I don't know. Where am I? Who are you?"

"I'm Dr. Turner. You're at Lancaster General Hospital. Do you remember what happened?"

A vision formed in Hannah's mind. Something big... and black... "A cow ran over me."

"It was a bull."

She turned to see Sam's face, very close. He was still holding her hand. "Sam?"

"I'm right here."

The tall woman in the white lab coat drew her attention. "I'm sending you over for a CT scan. Also for x-rays of your leg. You have an ugly contusion, but I want to rule out a fracture. Do you remember how you got it?"

Sam answered for her. "The bull kicked her in the leg. Her body was spinning like a top and she struck a light pole."

"Is that what happened, Ms. Rutledge?"

She nodded. "I think so."

A nurse appeared. The doctor gave her orders. Hannah's bed started moving. Sam still held on, very tightly.

"Sir, you'll have to stay here."

Hannah squinted at her friend as he released his grip.

"Will you be waiting when I get back?"

Sam touched her face. "Of course. Even if it takes forever, I'll be here for you. Always."

Chapter 9

D aisy sat on the bed, watching Jake sleep. They were in a motel in Rehoboth Beach. She had encouraged him to talk all day and night about his job. Daisy stood, brushing the hair from his eyes before returning to the mattress.

How doesn't he know? Jake was Mr. Right. She'd fallen in love with him when she was a kid. Been so hooked on Jake, she'd never even dated seriously. Her thoughts always came back to him.

Jake rolled in his sleep, stretching. The bright Delaware sun was peeking through the curtains.

When she'd seen him in college, she'd been too ashamed to speak with him. But even then, the fantasy of a life with Jake had been at the forefront of her thoughts. He was her inspiration, the reason to permanently lose her weight. To unleash the beautiful and confident version of Daisy she'd always believed she was. The one who'd been hiding inside.

Jake stirred, a dreamy, sleepy smile covering his face. He dozed back off.

God, you brought him back into my life. Like she'd always prayed would happen. And today, Daisy was hoping they could finally begin living, starting the romance she dreamed of.

Jake's voice startled her. "Morning, Daisy. Mind if I grab a quick shower?"

She felt her lips curl. He was so sexy, standing before her without a shirt. She wanted to take him in her arms, but instead replied, "Nope. Go for it."

The possibility that her dreams might actually come true thrilled her. Every cell in her body tingled. After the water stopped, Jake walked from the bathroom, drying his hair. He had donned a tank top, but his bulging biceps were showing.

"You ready for a fun day?"

Jake's face clouded. *Why?*

"Something wrong?"

His eyes sought hers. "What you did for me yesterday was really nice."

She laughed. "That's what friends do, help each other."

His face had a strange look, like something was bothering him, badly. *Losing his job?* He sat on the other bed, towel in his hands. "Exactly. Friends help each other." He appeared to study the carpet. His voice was soft. "You helped me, now I w-w-want to help you."

Curiosity filled her mind. "Help me how?"

Jake raised his chin until their eyes met. "W-w-with Mr. Right."

Daisy had to swallow, hard, before answering. "Do you think I need help?"

"Probably not, but please listen to me."

His eyes now seemed to glow. His lips so inviting. "Go on," she coaxed.

"I hope this comes out like I mean it. What would you think if I helped you with Mr. Right?"

The essence of his aftershave was so appealing. "What do you have in mind?" His face changed. *Is that longing I see?* "I'm listening."

Jake gulped hard. "I'd like to help you practice."

A chill dribbled down her spine. *Okay, that's a shocker.* "In what way?"

"W-would y-you mind if we pretended I was Mr. Right? You know, so when he does realize he loves you, you'll be prepared."

Oh my God. He really doesn't have a clue. "How would we do that?"

"Like, uh, just pretend I'm him. Of course, there's gotta be boundaries."

Daisy stifled back laughter. *Wait. This might be fun.* "What kind of boundaries?"

It was plain to see he hadn't thought this through. "Uh, like, uh, kissing for example. Maybe instead of kissing, we could rub noses."

Daisy stood and sat beside him on the bed. "Like this?" She gently rubbed her nose against his. The sudden desire to explore his lips was tough to fight off.

Jake pulled away. It was easy to see she'd excited him, too. "Yes."

"Are there other boundaries? What about holding hands?" She found his hand and squeezed it.

His breathing was rapid. "I think that's okay."

Just okay? She squeezed his hand tighter. "You sure? What other ones?" He returned the hand hug and quickly pulled away. He stood and walked to the edge of the bed.

"The big one. It's gotta be off-limits."

Daisy's face heated as the meaning sank in. "Yes, I agree with that. Anything else?"

"Uh, no. What do you think?"

She studied this man she wanted. *Doesn't realize I love him, yet.* She shot him her best smile as she extended her hand. "Agreed." He offered his hand and she pulled him close, again rubbing her nose against his. "You sure?"

Jake's head bounced up and down. "Absolutely."

"Great. Let's head to the beach, Mr. Right. Just let me slip into my beach clothes."

It only took a minute to change into the tropical themed bikini she'd brought. Daisy said a brief prayer before opening the door. His eyes widened as he drank her in. She handed him the sunscreen and turned away. "Mind rubbing me down?"

Jake's hands trembled as he oiled her shoulders. A giggle escaped her lips. *Jake Elliot, this might be your best idea yet.*

***

"Oh my God, Mom! Are you all right?"

Beth had opened the door for her. Hannah eyed her daughter, realizing she must look horrible. A glance in the truck mirror had revealed two black eyes. "I'm hurting, but okay." She used the crutches to get to the couch. "How did you get home?"

"Mrs. Campbell and Mrs. Miller—Ellie and Sophie—picked us up. What can I do to help? Make supper?"

Sam's strong voice filled the room. "Maybe you can help with Missi. I don't mind making supper, if that's all right."

Hannah turned to study Sam, comforted by his companionship today. "Thanks, Sam, but I'm sure you have more important things to do."

His eyes were filled with kindness. "Nothing's more important than being here, helping you."

Hannah happily sighed. While she'd waited for the results of the scan, she and Sam had talked everything out. He'd apologized, profusely, and explained what he'd been doing. His presence had helped make a bad day tolerable.

"Okay. I set out hamburger this morning. I was going to make beef stroganoff."

Sam nodded and walked to the kitchen. The look on his face was easy to read. He had no idea how to make it.

Beth brought some pillows and helped Hannah prop up her leg. Her eldest daughter played with her little sister while Hannah told her about the incident.

The clanging of pots in the kitchen drew her attention. Hannah raised her voice. "Everything all right in there?"

A loud crash followed. "Just peachy." Another bang. "I'm okay. I'll clean up when I'm done."

Before long, tasty aromas were coming from the kitchen. *Thank you, God, for helping us get past our problems.* Hannah had missed Sam, more than she cared to admit.

The kitchen door finally swung open. Sam carried a tray. Hannah stifled back a laugh when she saw the food. Sam had cooked the package of ground beef, whole, without breaking it up. Another bowl was filled with noodles in a lumpy sauce and a third contained carrots.

He sat it on the table and wacked off a hunk of meat, then slapped some pasta and veggies on the plate. His face was red as he handed it to her. "Hope this is all right."

Beth stared at him in horror. "You expect us to eat this?"

Hannah laughed for the first time all day. "I think it will be fine."

A knock sounded at the door. Beth opened it. Her neighbor John filled the opening and then rushed in. "Heard you got hurt, Hannah." His eyes caught Sam's figure. "Who the hell are you?"

His attitude irritated her. "This is my friend, Sam. Sam, that's John."

Sam nodded, but Hannah could sense the displeasure in his face. "Sir."

John strolled around the apartment as if he owned the place, again taking in Sam. "Thanks for helping Hannah. You can leave now. I'll take care of her."

Sam set the plate down and stood before John. "I don't think so."

John spoke to Hannah, but his gaze was on Sam. "Want me to escort him out?"

No, this is not going to happen. "Absolutely not. Sam's my friend. He came over and made us supper. Would you like to join us?"

John's stare took in the food. "I don't eat swill."

Sam's fists clenched momentarily before relaxing. Hannah expected Sam would have a comment, but he remained silent. Yet Sam didn't back away from the bigger man.

Hannah spoke up. "I think the food is fine. Now, if you don't want to join us, mind if we eat while it's hot?"

John's face turned red. "Fine. I know where I'm not wanted. When you change your mind about having the company of a real man, just knock on the wall." He turned and slammed the door on the way out.

Sam tried to hide it, but he was breathing hard. He turned to Hannah. "How else can I help you? Whatcha want... uh, I mean... what would you prefer to drink?"

Hannah didn't answer right away. It was as if a switch had turned on a light bulb. She suddenly saw Sam differently. As a man, not a kid. "I'd like ice water."

Sam cleared his throat. "Maybe I'll get you a glass and be on my way."

She relaxed as she watched him. "No. I want you to stay. After all, you did make supper." *And if I've got to eat it, you do too.*

Chapter 10

I s this a dream? Jake couldn't believe his good fortune. The night's ocean breeze carried with it the salty scent of the sea. A chill teased him from the cool air in direct contrast to the wonderful warmth of Daisy's fingers, gently entwined in his. The time was well after midnight and they had the beach all to themselves. The brilliance of a full moon lit up the night sky, trimming the clouds with a silver outline. For hours they'd just talked, about the shapes of the clouds, about their pasts, about life. About everything but their future.

"You still awake over there?" It was Daisy's voice, the sweetest one he could recall.

I think I'm in love. "Yep. How about you? Thought you might have dozed off a while ago."

Her giggle, like a mountain stream, filled his ears. "Believe I did. You had me so relaxed and the night sky is hypnotic. Hate for it to end, but I guess we should probably think about calling it a night. Somewhere, there's a mattress calling my name."

Jake rolled onto his knees so he could see her face. "Thank you for your kindness, for such a wonderful day."

The pearly whites of her smile glistened in the moon's light. "No. Thank you. This has been fun."

"Yeah. Good night." Her expression changed to one of bewilderment, but before she could answer, he stood and offered his hand.

Daisy's laughter drowned out the thunder of the waves. "I was worried for a second you might abandon me to the darkness."

"What? Leave a treasure like you out on the beach alone? Not a chance." She laughed once more. How could one girl be filled with so much happiness? It seemed to flow from every pore. *And how can she make my heart pitter-patter this way?*

She stood before him, brushing off the gritty Delaware sand. "I'm pretty tired. Mind driving?"

"'Course not." He offered his arm and escorted Daisy to her sedan, parked on the now deserted main drag. He held the door open for his yawning companion. Before they'd crossed the drawbridge, she was asleep. *Happiest day of my life.* Not even the best days he'd spent with his ex-wife Callie, when everything was right, could come close to making him feel like he did in this moment of time. *This is how it's supposed to be.*

The lights of the motel sign were bright when he parked the car. He turned and watched her sleep for almost twenty minutes. *She's gotta be an angel.* No matter what angle he saw her from, Daisy was perfect. In every way. So pretty, so kind, so full of joy and all the goodness in life. And the connection between them? *Like we're one.* His mind drifted to the future. Jake hoped this gamble would pay off, that she'd see him not just as a stunt double for Mr. Right, but as the real deal. The one she really wanted, for life. *Please God...*

Daisy shifted and yawned, arms curling around herself in a hug. "We're here? How long was I out?"

"Just a few seconds." He again opened her door, grabbed the beach bag and offered his arm. Once inside the room, he waited patiently while she showered. Daisy waltzed from the bathroom sporting a pink set of satin PJs—ones that complimented the crystal blue of her eyes. *She's so beautiful.* "Did you enjoy today?"

Her smile faded as she studied him. "It was perfect, except for one thing."

A chill crawled up his spine, like someone was walking on his grave. "What thing?"

She approached, sending excitement through his body as her fingers softly touched his chin. Daisy's nose was warm as she rubbed it against his. He almost fainted when she brushed against his lips. "It makes me wish this wasn't practice."

The taste of her lips set fire to his mounting desire. *Here's my opportunity.* Her blue eyes glistened. "Then let's make it real." He swallowed hard. "Let me make love to you." He lowered his lips toward hers.

Daisy's eyes flashed as she shook her head. Her hands were trembling but she roughly shoved him away. "No! Is that how little you think of me? That I'm just a fun time? How dare you! I am *not* that kind of girl. Good night, Jacob Elliot." Before he could respond, she found the way to her bed, wrapping herself tightly in the sheets.

Oh God, what did I do? He stood looking down on her frame. "I'm sorry. Didn't mean to…" A wall of silence answered him. *Crossed the line.* "I, uh, want to apologize. Can we talk about this?" Nothing, nada. "I don't want the night to end like this." Still nothing. *Idiot.* "I'm sorry. 'Night, Daisy." He grabbed his clothes and slunk toward the shower. His whole body trembled in anger, at himself. Should have treated her with respect, not like a tramp. *Why did I do that?*

***

The soft knock on the door rose Hannah from her slumber. *Why am I on the couch?* She started to move, but the pain radiating from her leg reminded her why. Because of yesterday's encounter. The incident with Sophie's cow. The one the bull won.

"I'll get it." Beth suddenly bounded across the room to open the door.

That's odd. Beth wasn't normally a morning person, usually requiring the threat of a crowbar to pry her from the bed.

Her daughter's body language said it all when the morning light filtered in behind the man standing there. Beth really liked the guy standing in the door frame. Her daughter's voice was flirtatious. "Good morning, Sam."

Sam Espenshade shuffled in, carrying several overflowing plastic bags. "Morning, Beth." He walked right past the girl. Beth cast a look of longing before closing the door. When her eldest headed back the hall, Sam turned to face Hannah. His brown eyes were smiling. "How you feeling, Hannah?"

She hurt, all over. "Like I got run over by a Mack truck. Did you get the license plate number?"

Sam's laugh was jovial. "Should have paid closer attention. Too busy checking you out... I mean, making sure you were okay."

Hmm. Something was different about Sam. She'd actually noticed it last night. *What was it?* Both his words and actions seemed different. "What are you doing here? You should be at work."

He set the bags down, uncapped a bottle of iced Frappuccino and handed it to her. "Figured today might be rough." Sam had such a great smile. "Thought you could use some company."

My favorite drink. He'd remembered. *Oh, Sam.* She took a sip and set it down before painfully pivoting to a sitting position. The chill of the liquid helped temper the warmth rising in her chest. Sam grabbed her crutches and offered them to her. "Thanks. Sam, you're supposed to be at the Campbell's. You don't have to babysit me. This was nice, but head to the farm. I'll be fine."

"Nonsense. I changed my shift. Don't have to be at work 'til one."

"Sam..."

"Oh, stop it. I brought breakfast. Just so you know, I *do* know how to cook, despite annihilating dinner last night. Give me another chance, please? With sugar on top?"

How can I resist? Hannah felt her lips curl. He hadn't ruined it. *Last night had been special, now that we're friends again.* Okay, it wasn't the tastiest food she ever had, but it wasn't the worst either. "Look, I've got to get Missi ready for the sitter."

Her skin tingled when his calloused fingers lightly touched her arm. "Let her stay home today. I'll watch over Missi."

Hannah's lips pursed as she studied this boy—no, young man—standing before her. "Sam, I'm not sure. I don't know if I can take care of her until Beth gets home from school."

"Got that covered."

"What?"

"It's a surprise. One you'll like, guaranteed."

Her fists balled. The one thing she hated was someone trying to run her life. She gritted her teeth to diffuse the mounting anger. "Don't you dare try to control me."

Sam laughed. "Never crossed my mind. I just wanted to take care of my friend." His face sobered and the words that slipped out were whisper quiet, but echoed like an explosion in her mind. "My *best* friend." He shifted slightly. "Hannah, if you really don't want me here, I'll go. It's up to you." He reached into one of the plastic bags and pulled a bouquet of red flowers. "I gotta tell you though, I'm hoping these might sway your opinion." To top it off, he shot her that crooked smile. *Missed seeing it.* The one he kept in his back pocket for those occasions when Hannah was angry with him. The expression she couldn't resist because it always made her smile.

She was suddenly light-headed. *Is it the flowers... or Sam?* The fragrance of those roses touched her in a way flowers never had before, once again spreading warmth across her chest. Feelings she thought had died along with her husband nibbled at the edge of her heart. "Your best friend?"

Sam nodded. "Of all time."

Time stopped. The distance between them shrank. He leaned toward her until they were all but nose to nose. As if in slow motion, he offered his hand. Hannah was but a spectator, watching her hand melt into his. It felt natural. *As if this is where I belong.*

"Samby!"

Hannah pulled away from him. The spell had been broken. Her friend dropped to his knees, arms open wide to catch Missi as she leapt at him. Then Sam stood and twirled the little girl in a circle as the pair laughed with abandon. The wonderful feelings in her chest intensified as Hannah took it in.

"Morning, Cinderella. Want to give Samby a hand making breakfast?"

Missi was trying to tickle him. "Make me chocolate chip pancakes."

With her daughter on his hip, he snatched the bags. "How 'bout a please?"

"Pwease, Samby?"

Sam shot Hannah a wink. "Be back soon, Mommy." He turned his head as Missi tussled his hair. "All right, princess. Special pancakes for you, and bacon and eggs for Mommy and Beth. I like your princess pajamas."

The door to the kitchen closed behind them, but their laughter seeped out. *Sam? Are these feelings real?* Hannah steadied herself on the crutches. Something deep inside her moved, trying to surface. It finally found its way into her heart. *Sam, you're my best friend, too.* Hannah's lips trembled as she listened to the laughs from the kitchen. *Of all time.*

Chapter 11

"Love you too, Mom." Daisy disconnected the call and dropped the phone back into her open purse. *That went well.* Vivian wasn't particularly fond of their ploy. Daisy's mind recalled her mother's displeasure.

"This feels like a very bad idea. Allowing him to pretend he's 'Mr. Right'? Mark my words, this is going to turn around and bite you."

"Why would you say that?"

"Daisy. A relationship built on a lie is doomed."

"It's not really a lie."

"No? Then what is it?"

"I don't know, Mama. It's a... a... a game. You know, so we can see how we'd get along. Like practice."

She'd felt, rather than heard, her mother's sigh. *"Sometimes I just don't understand your whole generation. But you're my daughter and I'll always trust you to make the best decision. Please be careful."*

Daisy took a sip of lukewarm coffee. *Best decision? Did I make a mistake?* She'd thought Jake was a good and honorable man. *Until last night.*

Good thing she didn't tell her mother about Jake's proposition. *"Let me make love to you."*

Maybe that wasn't any big deal to him. *But it is to me.* Maybe he hooked up with women all the time. *I waited all my life... for you.*

A seagull swooped down in front of her, landing on the dune. The bird picked through some trash, looking for food.

The bright sunshine was momentarily blotted out by a cloud. Suddenly, Daisy felt Jake's presence behind her on the boardwalk.

A pounding noise came from her left, intensified and receded to her right. Jogger's feet on the boardwalk. Daisy took a deep breath while she waited. *Help me, God. I'm not looking forward to this confrontation.* Another minute passed and he still hadn't shown his face. Her anger grew until she could no longer stand it. "Anyone ever tell you it's rude to stare?"

Silence. *Was I wrong?* Maybe he wasn't there at all. Before she could turn to look, his voice startled her. "Daisy, I'm sorry. I was trying to decide how to start this conversation. Can we talk about last night?"

She refused to turn around. "Maybe. If you can show your face."

He slowly walked around the bench and stood looking down at her. "Found your keys and your note. How'd you get here?"

Jake didn't look well this morning. Like he was restless, worried and tired. *Probably his conscience, if he has one.* "I took an Uber, so you could drive my car. So... something you wanted... besides sleeping with me?"

"Sorry. I wanted to..." Jake's voice trailed away.

"You wanted to what... talk to me? Then sit next to me, don't stand behind or above me. It doesn't make me feel good." Daisy ran her hand through her hair, turning toward the waves. "Of course, worrying about my feelings wasn't too high of a priority last night, was it?"

Jake sat next to her on the bench. She could sense him watching her face. "I screwed up."

Daisy turned to face him. "That's the understatement of the year."

He apparently couldn't look her in the eyes, but instead turned his gaze to the sea. He seemed to focus his attention on a freighter plodding along the horizon. The scent of his aftershave filled her senses, drawing her eyes to him. "Daisy, I care for you, a lot. But I didn't show it last night. Any way you can forgive me?" His hands were trembling.

"I'm disappointed you tried to take advantage of my kindness."

"I'm sorry..."

Jerk. Daisy's nose tingled and her vision blurred. She shook her head and turned away from Jake. "You treated me like some bimbo you picked up in a bar." Daisy brushed her cheeks. "So, you do this often?"

From the corner of her eye, she could see Jake shaking his head. "If you're talking about propositioning you or any other woman, the answer's no. If you mean making a colossal fool of myself, I need to warn you, it seems to happen quite frequently. Gave a great demonstration last night." Jake sat back against the bench, his head tilted skyward.

At least he didn't try to pretend he doesn't know why I'm upset. "Why'd you try to take advantage of me?"

He pivoted, reaching for her hand, but then stopped himself. "Yesterday was perfect. I just got, I don't know... I wish I could undo it, but I can't. I'm sorry."

"Jake, we agreed doing that was *not* an option."

He engaged her face, melting her resolve. His gaze was intense. "Yeah, let's talk about that."

Her eyes flew open. "What?"

He took a deep breath. "This whole pretending to be Mr. Right was a stupid, stupid, *stupid* idea. I give up. I think it would be best for me to head back to Pennsylvania."

Daisy's mouth fell open. "Are you serious?"

Jake's face was red and his eyes watery. He stood, hand fumbling in his shorts pocket. "Yeah. Here's your keys. What you did... nicest gesture ever. I'll be forever in your debt. Let me know how much this was, the motel, gas, all of it. I'll pay you back." His chin was trembling as he bit his lip. "Guess this is goodbye, Daisy." He placed the keys in her hand, then turned and walked away.

Wait! He was a man on a mission. By the time she'd gotten up, Jake was forty feet away and accelerating. "Jake, hold up." He didn't appear to hear her.

Her flip flops weren't the best footwear for moving quickly. Daisy abandoned them and ran barefooted to catch up.

Jake was in front of a café when she grabbed his arm. "Can you slow down already?" *Let me catch my breath.* There was a line outside and customers appeared eager to see what was going on.

"Sorry, Daisy. I'll have my stuff out of your room by the time you..."

Enough. She placed her hands on his chest. "Okay. You made your point."

His stare was one of bewilderment. "What point?"

She bit her lip before answering. "I might have been a little, uh, might have pressed the point harder than I should have."

Jake shook his head. "No, you didn't. I'm the one who's wrong. So disappointed in myself. All you showed me was kindness and I let my..." he hesitated, then grew quiet. He looked everywhere but at her. "I was wrong. I don't know how to fix this, so I guess the best thing for me to do is leave."

Daisy studied his expression as well as the feelings in her heart. *He's leaving for my sake, not his.* Time to salvage the moment. "Let's just stop for a minute. What's past is past. We have one last day before we head back home. Let's make up." She extended her hand. "Friends?"

Jake's frown was sad as his palm touched hers. "Friends." He looked away. "That whole pretending to be Mr. Right thing was dumb. We won't do that anymore."

Not letting you off the hook, yet. She placed her index finger against her chin. "Hmm. I don't know. I think I learned something here, uh, about how to handle Mr. Right. You know, if he steps over the line."

Jake exhaled sharply to make a point. "I'm sure he'd never do that. I can see in your eyes, he's perfect. Me? Not so much. About as far from perfect as a man can get."

Not as far as you think. Daisy cleared her throat. "Getting back to us practicing. Let's talk about it. So, Mr. Right has made a mistake and feels like a colossal fool. Yet, his dream girl has given him a chance to climb back on the pedestal he fell off. What happens next?" *Read my mind*.

He studied her intensely. Maybe she was wrong, but it was as if a light switch came on. "He takes her to an elegant breakfast?"

Um-hmm. Daisy nodded. "Okay, for starters. Then what?"

His eyebrows raised as he gauged her. "He tells her they can spend the day... doing exactly what she wants?"

Bingo. "Perfect. Let's go."

"Go where?"

"To get my flip flops. I couldn't chase you while wearing them. Then you can take me to breakfast, followed by outlet shopping."

Jake did a double take. "Shopping?"

Don't give in now. "Either that or we can stop practicing. Your choice."

He reached for her hand. "No, no, we'll keep practicing... you know, for the good of the cause. But there is one tiny little issue."

Daisy had to hold back the laughter building inside her. The good of the cause? *You and I are the cause*. "What's the problem?"

He squirmed, like a child afraid to confess he'd been wrong. "Uh, you may need to do a little coaching. Always hated shopping, but I'm willing to change. Please teach me how to shop. Daisy style."

Daisy felt her lips curl into a smile. "Good answer, Mr. Right. There might be hope for you, yet."

***

Hannah was so tired. After breakfast, the three of them played games until Missi grew disinterested and grabbed a Dr. Seuss book, *Green Eggs and Ham.* Her baby plopped on Sam's lap and he began reading to both of them. Sam's expressive and melodic voice lulled Hannah to the rim of slumber. She didn't protest when Sam helped her recline, removed her glasses and covered her with a blanket. *This feels so right.*

Suddenly, Hannah was removing pies from a box. A glance at the sign above the table impressed her, *Hannah's Bakery.*

"Mom, I'm gonna take the baby for a walk. Will you be all right for a couple minutes?"

Hannah drew a sharp breath. *Missi?* She knew the woman before her was her daughter, but Missi was all grown up. In her arms was a baby dressed in blue. *I have a grandson?* "Uh, sure, sweetheart."

Missi kissed her brow. "Be back soon. Maybe the three of us can grab some lunch when I return?"

Hannah nodded and watched the pair walk off. *How long was I asleep?*

An irritating voice startled her. "Thought she'd never leave." Hannah turned to discover Dale

Olphin wiping his finger across one of the pies. He licked the tip in a disgusting manner, then stepped closer. "Now, about you and me..."

Before she could move, another man's voice interrupted. "Move along, Olphin. We've talked about this before. Hannah doesn't want to see you and neither do I. Better take a hike... or maybe I should help you leave." Hannah turned to the source. *Sam?* He was much older. Above his tightly clamped lips, he sported a bushy gray mustache. The top of his head was shiny. *Sam's bald?* Sam rolled up his sleeves, revealing muscular arms as his fists curled. He stepped toward Dale.

"Sorry, Mr. Espenshade." Dale cringed and held his hands in front of him. "I, uh, forgot."

Sam threw his apron aside and walked toward the now cowering villain. "Remember quickly or I'll call the police. *After* I'm done with you."

"Okay, okay. I'm leaving." Dale turned and quickly disappeared into the crowd.

Sam turned to Hannah, softly taking her hand. "It's okay, honey. As long as I breathe, no one will ever make you feel that way again. I promise." His arms softly embraced her. "I love you, Hannah. Always have, and I always will."

Sam's lips were just about to touch hers. His scent thrilled her as she met his lips. They melted together. *Heaven.* Hannah had no idea where she ended and he began. Laughter erupted around her. Missi's laughter. Hannah's eyes flew open.

Sam's voice filled her ears. "You get in there and wash your hands, right now, princess." He held one of Missi's toys in the air. "I've got a bubble maker and I'm not afraid to use it."

"No, Samby!" Her daughter's laughter filled the apartment as she scampered to the bathroom.

When Hannah shifted position, it caught Sam's attention. "Hey there, sleeping beauty. How was your nap?" His smile was so magical.

A chill rolled over her. *Just a dream.* Hannah willed her heart to slow down, yet the taste of Sam's lips lingered on hers. *How can that be?* No, he was so young. "I'm, uh, was a good nap."

Sam held her glasses and offered his hand to steady her. But the electricity of his touch flowing through her increased her heartbeat. "Just in time for lunch. I'll fix the plates."

When his hand released hers, she could still feel his touch. She stared in wonder as he walked into the kitchen. *Is this real or just a fantasy?* Missi tore out of the bathroom, ignoring her mother as she chased after Sam. Everything was shaky when Hannah hoisted her body against the crutches and made her way across the room. Her reflection in the bathroom mirror mocked her. Two black eyes, hair askew. *How could anyone ever want me?* The voice resonating inside made her blush. She expressed it softly. "You know he does. He's in love with you." *No, just my imagination. I should fight this feeling.*

A knock on the door. Sam's sweet voice. "You okay in there? Lunch is ready."

She quickly washed her hands. "Coming, I'm coming." When she shoved open the door, she was in for a shock. Sam had the food all set out, as if it were a picnic. Roses were in a jar on the coffee table.

Is this another dream? The shakiness caused her to stumble and lose her balance. The floor rushed up to greet her.

"Whoa there, Hannah." Sam's strong arms caught her. He lifted her as if she were a pillow and carried her to the couch. The warmth of his breath against her cheek made her even dizzier. "Decided we'd have a little celebration." The cushions reached up to greet her as he gently sat her down. Sam groaned and plopped on the floor next to her. He was rubbing his leg when Missi jumped on his lap and tried to tickle him. "That's enough, Cinderella. Sit next to me. Time to say prayers."

The dream from earlier had left cobwebs in her mind. "What are we celebrating?"

Sam winked, drawing her attention to the depth of his irises. When he smiled, his eyes led the way. "No broken bones."

"What?"

"Yesterday could have been really bad." The sudden change in his expression sent a shiver up her spine. "Don't know what I'd do if you'd been hurt bad." *Oh my God! Could that be love?* His fingers brushed across the back of her hand. "I'm real sorry for treating you the way I did. I... uh..." An expression she'd never seen before covered his face. Sam leaned in until their foreheads were touching.

Hannah bit her lip as thrills filled her mind. *He's going to kiss me!*

"Do we hafta say prayers 'fore we eat?" Missi's words interrupted the spell. Again.

Sam's face broke into a big smile as he turned to the little girl. "Yep. You start." The warmth of his hand against her skin was making it hard to breathe.

"No. You do it, Samby."

"Oh, all right. Bow your head, Cinderella. God is great, God is good. Let us thank Him for our food." He hesitated. "And Father, please watch over Hannah and help her heal quickly. Take away her pain. Amen." He squeezed her hand once, very tightly before letting go.

Sam handed her a dish of fish sticks, peas, and macaroni and cheese. She realized there were only two plates, hers and Missi's. "Where's your food?"

He stood and walked over to grab his shoes. "Don't have time. Gotta get to work."

"But you didn't eat yet."

He laughed. "I didn't come over to eat. I came to be with you."

Just to be with me? "But aren't you..." A knock on the door interrupted her.

"Looks like the second shift's here."

What? "Who's there?"

"My replacements." Sam threw the door open. Ellie Campbell and Sophie Miller walked in, big smiles covering their faces.

Hannah was confused. "Uh, hi. What are you two doing here?"

Sophie carried in a large basket. "Sam asked us to visit until Beth gets home. I'm so sorry Oney hurt you."

"Oney? Who's that?"

"My bull. So sorry. How are you feeling?"

"I'm fine."

Sam's laughter drew her attention. "Right. Hannah's a little tired today. And still a bit unsteady." His smile disappeared as he walked over to touch her hand. "Thanks for a great day. Want me to come back?"

How about not leaving? "Sure. When?"

"Gotta work until three tomorrow. Come over after that?"

Please. "That would be okay, if you're not busy."

His smile returned and he nodded his head. "I'm never too busy to spend time with you. Thanks again for a great day. Goodbye." He grabbed Missi in his arms and blew bubbles against her neck. She howled with delight. "See ya, Cindee."

"Bye, Samby." Her girl gave him a kiss and then he walked out the door.

Hannah caught the look Ellie and Sophie shared. *Not just me. They saw it, too.* Ellie's voice was full of merriment. "Great guy, isn't he?"

Hannah simply nodded. *You have no idea.*

Chapter 12

Daisy plopped the stack of charts on her desk. The essence of pine from the air freshener usually lifted her spirit, but not today. She sat in her chair and swiveled around to the back table. The selfie she had taken of her and Jake at the beach caught her eye. His smile seemed sad. The photo had been taken the morning after the blowout between them. *Did I push too hard?*

The knock on her door drew her attention. Trenton walked in and handed her a bottle of diet cola. The man was always guzzling the caramel colored liquid. "Hey, Daze. You look a little down today."

She uncapped the drink. "No, I'm fine."

Trenton laughed. "Liar. Man trouble, that's what I think. Jake still acting like the fool he is?"

Her lips pursed. "No, and don't say that about him, not if you want to remain my friend."

He took a long swig of his Pepsi. "Oh, I see. Don't fret. You'll always be *my* friend." Trenton stared for a long moment. "You worry me. I'm wondering if Mr. Right might be Mr. Wrong for you, know what I mean?"

"He's not." She studied the face of her good friend. "You think I went overboard?"

"Let me ask you this. How did he make you feel?"

Daisy squirmed in her chair. "I don't know. Not good, I guess."

"Then the answer is no. Remember this, Daisy Mae, no one ever has the right to make you feel bad."

She was struggling with her thoughts. "But what if..."

Trenton grabbed her hand and drew her attention to him. His words were slow and measured. "No one ever has the right to hurt you, humiliate you or make you uncomfortable. Understand me?"

"I see what you're saying, but..."

"Hmm. Let's fast forward to today. How do you feel about him, now?"

"You know I love Jake."

Trenton emptied his bottle in one long swig and threw it into her trash can. She picked it out and handed the container back to him. "You are aware we have a recycling program in this building, aren't you? Don't just throw that away."

"Okay, tree hugger. I will... as soon as you tell me what's going on. You love Jake, but what... Come on, you can do it. Use your words."

Daisy stuck her tongue out. "Why do you always have to treat me like a child?"

"Because I think of you as my little sister. Speak."

Daisy's eyes gravitated back to the picture. "Ever since that morning, I feel like he's holding back. Maybe it's because he's worried about finding a job, but suppose it's not that. Maybe I went too far and hurt him."

"You didn't."

"Could it be the stress of looking for a job?"

"Maybe. How's that going?"

One of her nails had a nick. She'd caught it when closing a file cabinet earlier. "Good, I guess." She retrieved an emery board from the center drawer of her desk and worked on smoothing the rough spot.

"It's been over a month. Is he having success or not?"

"Oh, he's got quite a few companies interested in him, but the most enticing jobs are out of the area."

Trenton plopped down and propped his feet on her desk. "How far out of the area?"

"Atlanta. Chicago. But the one he likes the most is in Boston."

"And?" The following silence filled the room. "Man, this is like pulling teeth. Anything local?"

Daisy shot him the evil eye before continuing. "Not what he's looking for. Doesn't just want to be an engineer. He wants to be a manager."

"So if he did take a job a couple of hours away, what would you do? Would you move with him?"

Not about what I want. "Lancaster's my home. I really don't want to move."

"Then there's only one thing to do."

Daisy studied his face. "Enlighten me, oh wise one."

Trenton jumped to his feet and slammed his hands on her work surface. "Come on, girl. Tell him the truth. Let Jake know how you feel, that you want a life with him. That you're in love with him. Stop this stupid Mr. Right game and try honesty for a change."

You don't understand. "If I do that, he might turn his back on what he really wants to do... or worse yet, on me."

"Let me think about this. Jake has a choice. Either being some big shot in a firm or sharing a life with someone who loves and adores him. If Jake's as wonderful as you say, he'll make the right choice. I gotta tell you, Daze, if it was me and I was straight, I would choose you, every time. If he's got half his brain matter, he has to feel the same way."

My biggest fear. "Suppose he doesn't? Maybe it's all in my mind. Could it be he doesn't love me?"

Trenton shook his head as he turned to the door. "Never know if you don't try. I need to get back to my patients. Chin up and think about what I said."

After he left, Daisy again turned to the photo. "Do you love me, Jake?" Even though she willed it to, his reflection in the photo didn't change.

***

Hannah walked into the office where the time clock was located. Her leg still hurt. Even after therapy. After spending countless hours in Ellie's hot tub. She felt a smile fill her face. The quickness of the deep relationship that had developed with her boss's wife still amazed her. *Such nice folks.* Sam had been right. The Campbells were very good people. They were now her friends.

"Morning, Hannah." She turned to find the owner of the icy voice was Kyle. He was leering at her.

"Morning, Kyle. What's on the schedule today?"

His eyes narrowed. "I'm cleaning the fish tanks. You? How would I know? Hear you've been kissing up to Henry's wife. And because of that, Henry reassigned you."

Her mouth fell open. "What?"

He turned away. "You heard me. After all I've done for you. Thanks. Thanks for nothing, you worthless little twit."

The growl of a motor flowed in from outside. The door flew open and Sam waltzed in. "Morning, gimpy." His smile set off a tingling sensation in her chest. He swept off his hat and bowed. "Your chariot awaits you, m'lady."

What's he talking about? "I don't understand."

Somehow, Sam's smile grew. "Team Echo's back in town. You and me, we're weighing produce for Roots tomorrow. In hothouse seven, way at the end of the farm. Johnny and I are going to take you there."

"Johnny who?"

Sam held the door for her. "Johnny Deere." Before she could move, his hands were at her waist, lifting her onto the seat of the four-wheel drive utility vehicle. He stumbled slightly as he raised her.

"Sam, stop it. I'm too heavy for you. You're gonna hurt yourself."

"Don't worry. I'm fine. Let's get your seatbelt on." The touch of his hand against her hip as he fastened the belt made her warm all over.

Hannah whispered, "You're going to get in trouble. Quit making a scene. Everyone can see you."

Sam shrugged. "I don't care. Cleared it with Harry first. He said if anyone complains, let him know. He'll take care of it."

Sam climbed into the vehicle and turned to her. "Hold on. Here we go." He drove the utility vehicle slowly back to hothouse seven, parked it, turned off the engine and then jumped out. "I'll give you a hand."

"No, you won't. I'm quite capable..." He didn't give her a chance to finish as he again lifted her, gently placing her on the ground.

"There you go. See? Saved your energy. I'll help you get situated. Came in early and have everything set up for you."

This was nice, but I can't show it. "Please don't coddle me."

He shot her his easygoing smile. "I'm not doing that. I'm simply helping my best friend. On her first day back at work."

"I hope you're not going to act like this all day. I need to pull my weight. So what are we doing today?"

Sam pointed to a chair and a small bench. "Something new we started. We're pre-weighing and packing veggies. Should make the whole process go faster at the market."

"Sam. This doesn't seem very fair."

He laughed at her. "You'd do the same for me. Have a seat while I get everything set up." Sam disappeared toward the dock, before returning shortly. He was pulling a gaylord of grapes with a hand truck.

"So what exactly am I supposed to do?"

"Well, I'll put the fruit in a bag. You weigh it, print and attach the label, then hand it back. I'll pack the finished product."

She studied him. "How can that be fair?"

"Oh ye of little faith. Don't be such a pessimist. Need to learn to trust me."

Her chest warmed. *I do, very much.*

As the morning progressed, they packed grapes, cucumbers, tomatoes, onions and broccoli. Hannah had to admit, he'd set the process up in a very efficient manner. Not to mention in a way where she could prop up her leg and take it easy. When they broke for lunch, Sam again lifted her into the John Deere and drove to the main office building.

Sam helped her out and held open the door to the cafeteria. He touched her arm and she turned to him. "Got a couple of errands to run. See you after lunch."

Her heart sank a little as she watched him walk away. *I wanted to eat lunch with you.* Her feelings for Sam were confusing. She really cared for him, but a nagging voice told her to distance herself. *For his sake.* His whole life was ahead of him, while hers was probably half over. *Don't want to lead him on.* But her thoughts were interrupted. So many of her co-workers stopped over to say 'hello' she lost count. The caring these people displayed was genuine. No cattiness. No smart comments. *Like they're family.*

Before she knew it, Sam's voice caught her attention. "Okay, gimpy. Time to get back to work."

She shot him a look which she hoped was glaring. "Quit calling me that. You're limping today as bad as me. Maybe I'll call you gimpy."

His laughter was contagious and she couldn't hide her smile. He simply replied, "Copycat."

There was about an hour left in the shift when they finished weighing the product. Sam turned to her. "I'll go get the reefer truck. Be back shortly so we can load it up. You've been working hard, so take a break. Back in a jiffy."

His image receded from her view. His kindness and compassion moved her in a way she'd never felt before. *He's so nice to me. Why?* Sam had stopped by almost every day she'd been laid up, bringing or cooking food, ferrying her daughters places, playing board games with her and just spending time keeping her company. *Never had a friend like you.* Her mind was lost thinking about Sam until a foul smelling odor caught her attention. She turned to discover an angry looking Kyle facing her. He was wearing one of those paper suits... and boy, was it filthy. He had dark smears on his face. Sludge from cleaning out the fish tank.

"I see how it is. I bust my ass and you ride the gravy train. So this is what sucking up to the boss does, huh? Or was it more than that? Sleeping with the boss?"

Anger rose within her. "No. You're vile."

He stepped closer. "And you're a lazy bitch. And to top it off, they have your boyfriend baby you."

"My what?"

"Your boyfriend. Sammy Espenshade. The loser."

"Sam Espenshade? My boyfriend? Never. He's only a kid."

An evil laugh erupted from Kyle's lips. "Really? That's good. You need a man, not a boy." Kyle stepped even closer and she could smell it. Liquor. He was drunk. Fear gripped her heart. "A real man might do you good. I'll show you a thing or two." He grabbed the front of his paper suit and ripped it open.

Help me, please! The hothouse was at the end of the buildings. If she screamed, would anyone even hear her? "Help! I need help in here!"

Kyle grabbed her arm, yanked her from the chair and threw her onto the floor. Her leg screamed out in pain as she landed in an awkward position. He dug his fingernails into her skin. "No one's gonna help you. My turn, now."

An angry voice startled them both. "Get your hands off her right now!" Hannah glanced in the direction of the sound. The man's face was red and his hands curled into fists as he stepped closer.

***

Sam walked into the office so they could load up. *What a wonderful day, now that Hannah's back.* He was planning on taking her and her girls out to supper, as a celebration.

Harry looked up from the computer and nodded at him. The place smelled like gladiolas. *Yep, Harry's flowers.* He noticed a vase of them sitting on Harry's desk. Sam was very happy Ashley and Harry were together. The love between the pair was so sweet. *Looks like love is alive in Paradise.* Sam was contemplating when and how to tell Hannah he was in love with her.

Harry cleared his throat. "Need something?"

Sam couldn't help but smile. "Sorry, boss. Just grabbing the key to the refrigerator truck."

Henry's voice came from behind him. "How'd the new process go?"

Sam turned, noticing Henry rubbing the scar on his arm. Sam vividly remembered Harry telling the story of how Henry had rescued Miss Ellie when she'd been kidnapped. *Wish I could be a hero like Henry.* "I think it went pretty well. Guess tomorrow will be the test."

Harry nodded. "Works well. Increases efficiency. Sell more."

Henry laughed. "We'll see. By the way, how's Hannah holding up?"

She'd tried to hide it, but Hannah's tired. "She seems all right. I made sure she could sit all day, to rest her leg. I wish she would have taken more time off."

Henry nodded. "I agree. We'll stop back to check on her in a bit. I offered for her to work half-days, but she had her mind set on coming back full-time." The grin that covered Henry's face made Sam's cheeks warm. "I wonder why she was in such a hurry to return to work?"

Harry shook his head. "We all know why. Determined woman. Tired of her yet?" Harry's eyes had mischief in them.

Do they know... or are they teasing me? "Not at all." *I'd never get tired of being with her. Not in a million years.* "See you guys in a little bit."

Sam fired up the truck, drove to the hothouse and backed into the dock. He had just walked in when he overheard Hannah's voice. "Sam Espenshade? My boyfriend? Never. He's only a kid."

He shut his ears to the rest of the conversation. Sam shivered. *After all I've done and she only sees me as a kid.* He needed some fresh air. Sam was almost on the dock again when he heard Hannah scream, "Help! I need help in here!"

He rushed in to see Kyle yank her from her chair and throw her to the floor. Sam caught Hannah's grimace of pain. Sam and Kyle had a past. Kyle was a bully, and a nasty one. In high school, Sam had stood up for a defenseless girl Kyle was bullying. Kyle had won that fight, but at least he left the girl alone after that.

Sam was seeing red. "Get your hands off her right now!"

Both Hannah and Kyle stared at him as if in shock. A nasty smile slowly covered Kyle's face. The man grabbed Hannah's arm and twisted until she cried out in pain. "Man enough to make me?"

Sam sprang forward, landing a hard punch to Kyle's eye. Kyle released Hannah. Sam grasped Kyle's filthy shirt and threw the bully to the floor. To Sam's surprise, Kyle immediately jumped to his feet, grabbed a nearby two-by-four and swung it hard.

Pain exploded in Sam's leg, right where the pins held his bones together. Sam shuddered when he heard his bone snap. The room started spinning. Stars filled Sam's vision. The pain was intense. He tried to balance himself on his good leg, but before he could respond, Kyle swung the board again, striking the side of Sam's face.

His head slammed onto the concrete. Suddenly, Kyle was on top of him, rolling Sam onto his back. "Never learned your lesson, did you, Espenshade?" Kyle wrapped his hand around Sam's neck and proceeded to pound Sam's face with his fist.

Sam tried to get up, but another blow drilled his head hard against the floor. Everything was violently spinning. Sam was helpless to defend himself.

As if from a distance, he heard Hannah yelling, "Stop it! Help! Help!"

Kyle continued the beating, until it suddenly ceased. Sam forced his eyes open, but didn't know if the sight was real or not. Kyle was suspended in the air, hands grasping at his throat, legs flailing.

A voice called out. "Damn you. Woman told you to stop, didn't she?" *Is that Harry?*

The room was one big whirlpool. Kyle's body slammed against a support beam as a man held him there. *It is Harry.*

"Put him down, Harry," came a new voice. "I don't need my brother thrown in jail for murder. Kyle, leave. You're fired." Henry Campbell was by Sam's side, gently touching Sam's shoulder.

Out of nowhere, Hannah appeared on his other side. "Sam, Sam. Are you okay? Talk to me, honey. Please?" Her voice was coming in bursts. Hannah's cheeks were wet.

From the corner of his eye, Sam observed Harry throw Kyle to the floor. Again, Kyle jumped to his feet, but this time faced Harry. "Make me leave, limey. If you think you're man enough."

Harry's face turned red as he stepped closer to Kyle. "My brother said you were fired. What part of get off our property, quit breathing our air and never return didn't you understand? Or maybe I should thrash you to within a quarter-inch of your life. How's that grab you?"

Henry jumped up and grabbed Kyle by the hair. In disbelief, Sam watched him drag a screaming Kyle away.

Hands were touching Sam's face. He heard a voice. *Hannah?*

"Sam, stay with me, please. Talk to me. Sammy?"

His vision darkened. A familiar face appeared before him. Sam reached for it. One word left his lips before everything grew dark. "Jenna?"

Chapter 13

T he knock on his door brought him back from the valley he'd wallowed in all afternoon. *That late already?* The digital display on his watch read 4:02. *Daisy's here early? I'm not ready.* Jake had been sitting at the computer for the last ten hours, working on getting a job. He was still dressed in shorts and a t-shirt. *I'm such a pig. Haven't even showered yet.* He opened the door, amazed, as always, at how beautiful she was. "Hi, Daisy. Come in. Didn't realize what time it was."

"That's okay. I left a little earlier than normal. I'd had enough and besides, I couldn't wait to see you." She reached up and rubbed her nose against his. He quickly pulled away. "That's what you're wearing tonight? Did you forget we're going to a hockey game?"

Rats! It had slipped his mind. Dinner and a game... that's what he'd promised her. "Actually, it did. Give me ten minutes and I'll be ready."

Daisy moved the papers from the easy chair to the table, sat down and extracted her phone from her purse. "How was your day?"

Jake gulped. He didn't really want to tell her what transpired, but then again, it probably didn't matter to her at all. "I'll fill you in later, maybe during the drive to Hershey. And your day?"

She sighed. "Exhausting. I was more of a babysitter than a manager."

"What do you mean?"

"Trenton took off this afternoon. Some of his nursing staff were very liberal in the length of their breaks. When I tried to prod them back to work, one RN told me in very explicit terms I wasn't her boss." Daisy waved her hand. "Just annoying, that's all. Go and get ready. I'll be waiting." Her smile was so pretty. *How will I be able to live without seeing it every day?*

"I'll hurry." He stopped in the bedroom and grabbed his clothes. Next stop was the bathroom for a shave and shower. He studied the reflection of the man in the mirror. "You're the stupidest guy I know. For suggesting this foolish game and worse yet, for allowing yourself to fall in love with Daisy. Finally, for even dreaming she'd ever care for you." After rinsing the shaving cream from his face, he caught another glimpse. "Such an idiot. Going after a job you don't want, just to get away from the girl you do want." *World's biggest fool.*

***

Daisy pretended to check out the texts on her phone, but gave up. *Something's wrong.* Jake had pulled away so quickly when they rubbed noses. Maybe Trenton was right. Perhaps honesty would be the best choice. *But how?*

Daisy walked to the window. The leaves on the Tree of Heaven along the road were turning color.

What should I say? She whispered softly to herself. "Uh, Jake? Just wanted to say I love you and want to marry you?" No. "How about, 'you're the man of my dreams'?" Even worse. "I've been in love with you since the day we met, when I was thirteen and don't want to live another day without you." *Yeah, right.*

The movement of the curtains when the heater turned on interrupted her thoughts. Both her mother and Trenton were right. Pretending there was a Mr. Right besides Jake was wrong. *I need to tell him, but when?* Her heart screamed the response. *Tonight.* But how?

A pinging noise drew her attention. It was Jake's laptop. His e-mail was open. From this distance, she couldn't determine what the popup window said. The noise from the bathroom told her he was still in the shower. The temptation to read his e-mail forced her feet toward the device. *He'll never know.* The inquisitiveness of her mind egged her onward.

But her conscience won out. Daisy verbalized her thoughts. "No, stop it. I refuse to do that." She forced herself back into her seat.

"Stop what?" Daisy turned to find Jake standing in the doorway, drying his hair. Even his old, worn blue jeans and an ancient Hershey Bears jersey couldn't hide his muscular build. Her eyes met his. It was easy to see the curiosity behind those windows to his soul. "What'd you say?"

Her palms were suddenly sweaty. "Uh, I don't know. I'm kind of scatterbrained today." She forced a giggle out. "Never know what you get with me. Sometimes random words just dribble out of my lips. I was probably thinking about Trenton's crew."

He flashed an expression that said 'I don't believe you', but another one took over. It looked like sadness. *Why?*

Jake turned away. "Whatever. Gotta get my shoes on, then I'm ready."

Daisy followed him to the door frame of his bedroom. "We've got plenty of time. Mind stopping by to see my aunt and uncle before the game? They're at the nursing home in Blue Ball. We can catch Route 322 and head to Hershey afterwards. It's their sixty-first anniversary."

He nodded. "Sure. We can take as long as you like. We can grab food at the Giant Center in between periods instead of hitting a restaurant, if you want."

"I like that idea. I love those salads we get from that stand behind the visitor's goal. Would you like to eat there?"

Jake grunted. "Sure."

Daisy drove, as she usually did. She loved her little Fusion, but hadn't told Jake what she'd named it. From before they'd reconnected, she called the little Ford the 'Jakester'—in his honor. There was an uncomfortable silence between them today and she couldn't understand why.

Jake seemed to be particularly interested in the landscape. He pointed out the window. "Look at the color on those mums. Fall's my favorite time of year. What's yours?"

Anytime you're near? "Spring's my favorite season. Especially when it rains. Seems like there's a million shades of green on the trees and the world is so full of promise... and of course, flowers.

Speaking of flowers, have you ever been to Longwood Gardens? There must be millions of flowers there. If you'd like, I'd love to take you there. But the season doesn't really matter. It's so beautiful there, any time of year."

"Yeah. I went there once."

She caught the sad expression on his face. Was it sorrow? *Bad memory from Callie?*

The silence returned. Daisy prayed as she drove. *Help me say this right. Plant the right words in my heart.* But they didn't come. She was so lost in thought that she missed the turn to the nursing home and had to backtrack. Jake either didn't notice or else wasn't in a hurry. Normally he teased her about everything. Not tonight.

Once parked, he didn't even hurry over to open her door, as he always did. Head down, Jake followed Daisy into the building. The odor of food mingled with the other, less desirable odors which always seemed to be present. The room her aunt and uncle shared was empty. A nursing assistant told her they were in the common room.

She led the way, with Jake a few steps behind. And there they were. Holding hands, sharing a blanket as Uncle Harold talked away. A smile filled Daisy's lips. Uncle Harold was the storyteller of the family. Always had been. He could describe a mundane trip to the grocery store in such a way to make you believe it was a harrowing adventure. Daisy walked in front of them. "Happy Anniversary, you two."

Her Aunt Lena's face broke into a big smile. "Harold. Look who's here. Our Daisy, prettiest flower in the world." Jake stepped up beside Daisy. "And who is this? Is he the man you've been telling us about?" Before Daisy could utter a word, her aunt said, "Nice to meet you, Mr. Right."

Daisy's face heated. *Not yet. I need to tell him first.* "Uh, this is my good friend, Jake Elliot. Jake, my Aunt Lena and Uncle Harold."

"Hi. Pleased to meet you." But as Jake extended his hand, Daisy couldn't help but notice it was shaking. She glanced at his face and was suddenly filled with concern. His vibrant eyes seemed to change right before her. They were now vacant. *Why?*

***

After Sam lost consciousness, Hannah was frantic. She kept shaking him. "Sam, Sam. Are you with me?" Blood was oozing out of his nose. She grabbed a rag used for cleaning fruit and applied direct pressure.

Harry knelt next to her. "Called an ambulance for him. Are you hurt?"

Doesn't matter. "I think I'm okay, but I hope Sam's not hurt too bad."

Harry pointed at Sam's calf. Hannah hadn't noticed the strange angle at which it was bent. "Think he might have a broken leg."

She swallowed hard to keep her sob inside. In the distance, she could hear the wail of an ambulance. Suddenly, Henry stood before her. "Hannah, Ellie's on her way. She'll take you to the ER."

"No, I want to go with Sam. I don't want him to be alone."

"He won't be alone. Ellie got ahold of his mum. She'll meet him at the hospital." Henry touched her arm. "I'm concerned about you, too. Come, let's get over here and have you sit down. Sam's not the only one who's suffering. You are, too."

Her vision blurred. Hannah had to peel the cloth off her hands. A sob escaped. *Please wake me from this nightmare.* Her fingers were sticky from blood. Sam's blood. The voice startled her. It took a moment for her to realize it was hers. "Watch over him. He's my best friend. Heal him, please."

Harry ran outside to meet the paramedics while Henry helped her sit down. He stripped off his coat and covered her shoulders with it. "Sam will be fine. I guarantee it."

My world's ending. Hannah's words came out choppy. "He rescued me. Kyle was drunk and nasty, but Sam, he... he saved me. Never had a friend like Sam. What would I do without him? I need him, Henry."

Henry was on his knees in front of her, watching her eyes. "I know you do. And I hope you realize he needs you just as much. You do, don't you?"

I need to be at his side like he was for me. Suppose he wakes up and I'm not there? Hannah tried to get up, but her boss didn't allow it. "Let me go with him, please? My leg's fine, really. I'll go crazy if you don't."

Henry held her hands. "I can't do that. It's not your physical health I'm worried about. I'm concerned about shock. That's why Ellie will take you in to the hospital. My wife's your friend. You need to be with a friend right now."

Friend? My best friend is there, on the ground. Her eyes drifted to the man lying on the floor. She pointed at the motionless body. "He's my friend."

The sound of Harry's voice filled the room as he pulled the stretcher in. "Come on, boys. Put your heart into it." The two paramedics seemed to be rushing to keep up as Harry dragged them along.

"Please be careful with him," Hannah whimpered.

A sweet fragrance filled her lungs as warm arms wrapped around her. Ellie had arrived. "Come on, Hannah. My truck's right outside. I'll help you."

"No, Ellie. Sam... he... he needs me."

"Yes, he does. That's why I'm going to make sure you're okay." Ellie turned Hannah's chin until they were eye to eye. "He's gonna need you when he wakes up, so let's make sure you're okay," she repeated. "And don't worry about your girls. Sophie went to pick them up. Henry and I think it's best for all of you to stay with us tonight."

"No, I can't impose... I want, no... I need to be with Sam."

"Okay, we'll arrange that as soon as we can, but we need to take care of you first."

The medics elevated the stretcher. Foam blocks supported Sam's neck. It felt like Hannah's life was over. *Don't take him like You took my husband. Please? I need him.*

Chapter 14

J ake's mind wandered as Daisy drove toward Hershey. Seeing the closeness of her aunt and uncle touched him, deeply. Holding hands, laughing and joking as if they were just married. Even after sixty-one years. He'd finally seen true love with his own eyes. *Why couldn't that be Daisy and me?* Not the old part, but the love.

A swath of green, orange and brown caught his vision. Pumpkins still on the vine. The memory of his mom and dad carving jack-o-lanterns with him filled his mind. How they would line the sidewalk with their masterpieces. Some were scary, but most were plain funny. The taste of toasted pumpkin seeds was on his tongue. A hole opened in his chest. *Never gonna have kids to share life with.*

"You're pretty quiet over there." At Daisy's comment, the vision faded.

"I was looking at the pumpkin field we passed. Remembering Halloween when I was a kid. Doesn't it seem like when you're younger, the entire calendar is filled with holidays? At least it was for me. Now what's left? Work. Or in my case, finding work." *Need to break it to her.*

"I hated October. My brother used to terrorize me with ghost stories and make me watch horror movies with him. And you."

Jake grunted. "Never liked those type of movies. Only watched them with you two because I knew you were scared silly."

Daisy's laugh. *The sound of Heaven.* "You've always enjoyed picking on me, haven't you?"

He nodded. "It's been fun." *Actually, I loved every second of it.*

"Then don't act like it's in the past. You seem down this evening. Would you like to talk about it?"

"Later. Just want to enjoy tonight and not think about my problems."

He jumped when she took his hand. "Okay, we can talk about it later, if you'd like. You do know I'll always be here for you, don't you?"

Jake's vision became blurry. *Tonight's the last night.* He couldn't go on like this for her sake, or for his. It was time to let her go. "Yep."

The warmth of her hand felt so right, so natural. *That Dr. Rohrer's such a lucky man.* He had to be Mr. Right. Jake just knew it.

"Are you busy tomorrow, at lunch?"

"Don't have anything scheduled."

Her hand suddenly trembled. "Tomorrow at lunch, I'm going to introduce you to Mr. Right. It's time to let him know how I feel. That I'm in love with him. And I need you to be there."

Jake clenched his jaw and stared out the window with bleary eyes. "Okay. Just let me know when and where." *I won't be there... couldn't take it.*

"Let's meet at the Tea Room, at noon."

"Sounds good."

The rest of the drive was in silence. *At last this ludicrous game, and the torture, will finally end.* They arrived at the Giant Center. Jake pulled out his wallet and handed her a twenty. "I'll pay for parking."

She giggled. "My treat."

Jake was surprised at the gruffness of his own voice. "No. You drove. I asked you to come here, so I'll pay."

Her eyes widened. "If you insist, Mr. Right."

"Don't call me that, anymore. I'm tired of this stupid game."

Confusion filled his mind when she shot him a smile. "I am, too."

Without another word, they parked, passed through Security and found their way to their 100-level seats. He tried to concentrate on the pre-game activities, but couldn't. His heart was breaking. After a scoreless first period, they joined the throng and stood in line for their salads. Daisy had converted him from being a meat and potato man to one who now loved salads. She was such a great chef. *Just another thing I'll miss about her.*

Hershey scored three times and had a two-goal lead midway through the third period. Jake could have cared less. His mind was filled with the memories they'd made. *My life's ending.* He was startled when Daisy shook his arm. "Look. They're doing the Kiss Cam." On the big screen, the camera man would focus on couples and watch them kiss. Suddenly, Daisy's face was on the screen, along with his.

Jake turned to Daisy. He'd never seen anyone's smile as beautiful as hers. She leaned toward him. His heart seemed to stop. Her lips were so close, he could feel her breath. The way her eyes sparkled... Daisy's voice was barely a whisper. "Kiss me, Jake."

***

The adrenaline was gone. Hannah's ankle throbbed. They had taken two sets of x-rays before determining it was only a severe sprain. She hobbled out to the waiting room wearing an air cast and using crutches. Again. *Hate these things.*

Ellie stood when she caught sight of Hannah. "Is it broken?"

The pain in her ankle was nothing compared to the misery in her heart. "No. You hear anything about Sam?"

The expression on Ellie's face changed slightly. "Just spoke with Harry. He's keeping Sam's mom company." Ellie looked down. "Sam's been in surgery for a while."

"His leg or his head?"

"For his leg. Kyle snapped Sam's bone, right where it was broken before."

Because of me. The world was suddenly unsteady. "I don't feel so good. I'm really dizzy."

Ellie was at her side immediately. "We need some help over here!" Two nurses appeared, transferred Hannah to a chair and checked her vitals. After a few minutes, the nurses told Hannah she was fine and could still go home, but they brought a wheelchair to take her to the car.

As soon as Hannah was seated, she turned to Ellie. "I want to see Sam."

Ellie frowned and shook her head. "You can't. He's in the operating room. Harry and Sam's mom will be there for him when he wakes up."

"Ellie, please. I want to be there when he wakes up, too."

"What about your daughters?"

Between her injury and Sam being hurt, Hannah had forgotten about them. Guilt filled her. "I, uh, you're right. But can we at least stop by and see if he's out of surgery? It's important, Ellie. To me."

The compassion on Ellie's face was easy to see. *Such a great friend.* Ellie changed direction and navigated the corridors until they were in the waiting room where Harry was seated with a very attractive brunette. She didn't appear to be much older than Ellie or Hannah.

Harry jumped to his feet. "Hannah. Anything broken? You've got a cast on."

"No. I'm okay. Just a sprain. Any word on Sam?"

"Not yet."

The brunette approached her. Her resemblance to Sam was remarkable. *His sister?* Hannah was surprised when the woman hugged her. "Hello, Hannah. Glad to finally meet you."

Her fragrance was of late spring flowers. "Finally meet me? How do you know who I am?"

The brunette offered her hand. "I'm Rhonda, Sam's mom. I recognized you from the pictures my son took of you. Harry said you were hurt, too."

She looked so young. *Sam's mom?* "I'm okay, I guess. Your son, he saved me. I, uh…"

"Of course he did. Sam talks about you all the time. You're so important to him. You and your daughters. But he held back. You're even prettier than he described."

Hannah's cheeks heated. "I don't know what to say. Thanks. How is your... son?"

Rhonda's face clouded. "Still in surgery. The doctor is trying to pin his bone back together. His leg is broken, right where it was before."

Hannah's heart raced. "Before? Is that why he limps?"

Rhonda nodded. "Thought he would have told you by now. He was in a bad car accident a little over two years ago. His femur was crushed. Ruined his career."

His career? "I don't understand."

A sad smile took its place on Rhonda's lips. "I see Sam has lots of things to fill you in on. But Sam should be the one to tell you, not me. The doctor told us my son also has a bad concussion and a broken nose." Rhonda studied Hannah's face.

Hannah could feel hot drips of liquid on her cheeks. She couldn't keep the sorrow inside. "I'm sorry."

Rhonda dried her tears. "Don't be. This wasn't your fault."

"Do you know when he'll be out of surgery?"

Harry answered, "The nurse stopped by a few minutes ago to give an update. It's gonna be a while. You need rest. We'll call you... Oh... That's right. You don't have a phone." Harry scratched his chin and then held his finger in the air. "I forgot. Henry said you'd be staying at our house tonight. I'll keep Ellie updated and she can let you know the minute he hits recovery."

Hannah didn't want to leave. While her body might go, her heart and thoughts would stay with Sam. Ellie handed her a tissue to wipe the moisture from her eyes. *Please, God...*

Rhonda hugged her again. "You go now, with Ellie. The Campbells, they'll take care of you. And I'll make sure Sam knows you were here."

Hannah hesitated. "I guess that's okay. Please tell him I asked about him and that I said..."

Rhonda's expression was full of understanding. "That you said what?"

Hannah swallowed hard. She couldn't say it, not in front of everyone, not without Sam hearing it first. "That, uh, that his best friend needs him and I need him to get better."

Rhonda nodded. "I will, dearie."

After saying goodbye, Ellie wheeled her back to where the SUV was parked. Hannah's mind reflected on the words that hadn't left her lips. *Tell him I love him.*

Chapter 15

Daisy's entire body trembled with anticipation. The dream she'd fantasized about for years was finally going to come true. Jake was going to kiss her. She closed her eyes. A wave of shock rolled over her when his lips brushed her forehead. She opened her eyes and saw him pull away. People around them were booing, because he didn't kiss her on the lips. His jaw was set and he looked down at the rink.

Daisy touched his arm. "I thought you were going to kiss me."

Without looking at her, he answered. "I did."

"You know what I meant. Why didn't you?"

"We agreed kissing on the lips wasn't an option."

The vibes coming from him were not good. "That was when we were playing the game. Thought you wanted to quit?"

"I did. Doesn't matter." He suddenly turned to her. "The Bears have this one in the bag. Mind if we head back to Lancaster?"

Her trembling fingers touched his arm. "Don't you like being with me anymore?"

He stared at her with near lifeless eyes. "I need to tell you something."

"Go ahead. Like I told you, I'll always be here for you."

Jake's jaw was set as he shook his head. "Not now. When you drop me off."

Her body trembled. *Is he going to dump me?* No. She had to stop this train before it wrecked. "I have something to tell you, too. I was going to wait until tomorrow, but maybe I'd better do it tonight."

Jake's eyes moistened. He quickly grabbed his coat and stood. "I need some air. Take your time. You can watch the whole game if you want, I don't care." Without another word, he worked his way down the aisle and ran up the stairs.

Daisy swallowed hard. *What happened?* She couldn't understand why he was so upset. Then it hit her. *He still thinks someone else is Mr. Right.* She couldn't let this go on. Daisy was going to tell him as soon as they got in the car. It took a few minutes to mentally prepare herself. Butterflies nibbled on her insides. *Tonight's the night!* Daisy was anticipating the joy of being in his arms, seeing the love on his face.

There were two minutes left in the game when she headed out. The brisk evening air filled her lungs as she stepped outside under a galaxy of bright, living stars. Not a cloud in the sky. Such a beautiful night. Before she made it to the parking lot, Jake was there. Her heart was in her throat.

"Hey, Jake. Did you see those stars?"

"No." Even in the parking lot lights, she could tell he was horribly upset. "I need to tell you something, Daisy."

Her shoulders tingled as a chill climbed her spine. She started to walk past him. "It's chilly. Let's talk in the car."

He grabbed her arm and spun her around. "No. I want to say this now."

She was confused. Daisy's hands were shaking. "O-okay."

He looked everywhere but at her face. "No easy way to say this. I took the job in Boston."

What? No! "I don't understand. Thought you were still in the early stages of the interview process and... and now... You took the job? Without talking to me?"

His jaw was quivering. "Don't make this harder than it is. They're flying me up to look for housing this weekend."

No, God, no! "Jake, please. There's something I need to tell you first."

He shook his head. "Just wanted to say goodbye." He grabbed both her hands.

It was suddenly hard to breathe. "I don't want your goodbye. Let's talk about this, and us, on the way home."

"I called an Uber. You've been a Godsend and..." he sobbed, hard. "I'll never forget you."

The crowd started to flow out of the stadium. The volume of noise was deafening.

Before she could get a word out, he pulled her to him and kissed her in the way she'd hoped for earlier. The world rolled away as his lips caressed hers. When he broke the embrace, it was hard to stand. But just as quickly, he ran across the parking lot in the direction of Hockersville Road.

Her voice didn't seem to want to come out. She yelled after him, "Jake, wait. Don't leave me. I love you, Jake. Come back!"

But he didn't seem to hear. He kept running away. Daisy fell to her knees, the briskness of a sudden wind chilling the wetness on her cheeks, under the canopy of cold, lifeless stars.

Chapter 16

"Mom. Wake up. Wanted to give you a kiss before Harry and Ashley drop me off at school."

Hannah's mind was fuzzy. Must have been the painkillers. "Why would they pick you up here at home?"

Beth's lips brushed her cheek. "We're not home. Sophie brought us here last night. Don't you remember? We're at Ellie's house."

"Wait. What?"

"Gotta go, Mom. Don't want to be late. See you here, tonight."

Just like that, Beth was gone. *Missi?* Hannah threw off the covers and pivoted. But when her ankle hit the floor, the pain was excruciating. "Ow! Good Lord, that smarts."

"Morning. Need a hand?" Ellie walked into the room. She grabbed those hated crutches and held them for Hannah.

"Where's Missi?"

Ellie laughed. "In the kitchen, being royally spoiled by Mum."

"Mum? Who's that again?"

"Henry's mother, I'm sure you remember her. Her name is Darcy, but we all call her Mum. She has breakfast ready. And my brother-in-law Harry's teasing your daughter to no end."

Hannah's mind was starting to settle. *Sam!* "Harry's here? Does that mean Sam's out of surgery?"

"Um-hmm. About four this morning. I tried to wake you, but you were dead to the world."

"Ellie, I need to see him. Can you take me there?"

Ellie brushed her hair from her eyes. "We can go, but let's get some food in you first. Mum has bacon, sausage, potatoes and eggs ready." Ellie giggled. "You might want to grab a shower before we visit him, after you eat." Ellie pointed to a second door from the bedroom. "Shower's in there when you want it. Sophie grabbed clothes for the girls, but forgot about you. We're close to the same size, so I'll open my wardrobe to you."

"This is nice, but..."

"Nonsense. Hannah, come on. We're friends. You'd do the same for me."

Probably not. "You're so kind. Why'd you bring me here last night?"

Ellie's face sobered. "Henry thought it might be a rough night for you. Not just physically, but emotionally. He thought you might be a little worried, because of what Kyle did. And besides, we loved having your girls. Mum colored with Missi while Ashley and Henry got a lesson in air hockey from Beth. Missi's pictures have the place of honor on our fridge."

"I see."

Ellie studied her. "Want some help or do you just want to come out when you're ready?"

Hannah felt her face heat. What the Campbells had done was so thoughtful. Friends like this were hard to come by. Her heart suddenly ached for her best friend. *Sam.* "Let me get my bearings and I'll be out shortly."

"The dining room is down the hall to your right. We'll get your plate ready. OJ or coffee, or both?"

She was shaky. Hannah hadn't eaten since yesterday at lunch. "Maybe both?"

Ellie winked at her. "Gotcha. Yell if you need anything." Her friend left the room.

Hannah replayed yesterday's event in her mind. *Are you okay, Sam?* She vaguely recalled meeting his mother. *Was her name Rhonda or Rhoda?* Didn't matter. She had to see Sam, as soon as she could. Had to know he was doing all right. There was a devastating emptiness in her chest. *Is what I'm feeling real?*

Hannah had a hard time balancing, but she finally found her way into the dining room. Ellie was sitting in a chair, nursing the baby. Noise was coming from the kitchen, probably Darcy.

A steaming plate of food awaited her. Her eyes gravitated to the wonderful little girl stuffing her mouth with pancakes. Missi. Her daughter's voice was choppy as she talked and chewed. "Mommy. I like it here. Mumsy made me chocolate chip pancakes, just like Samby does."

Hannah hobbled over and wrapped her arms around her baby. Missi's lips were sticky when the little girl kissed Hannah's cheek. "Love you, Mommy."

Just like Samby does. Her face blanched. *Am I thinking about pancakes, or his love?* Hannah's words were choked by her emotions. "I love you, too."

***

Sam's eyes opened. His mother was by his side, holding his hand. "Hey there, sleepy head. I was wondering if you were going to sleep the day away."

He was in a white room with lots of medical equipment. His heart sank. Just like before. "Where am I, Mom?"

"Lancaster General. Pretty rough day for you, yesterday. What do you remember about it?"

The day slowly replayed in his mind. The joy of being with Hannah, then the heartbreak of the words she'd spoken. *"He's only a child."* The confrontation with Kyle briefly crossed his thoughts. *Kicked my ass, again.* Then Jenna's face had appeared. *Thought I was gonna join you, sis.* He focused on the wall.

Rhonda's voice interrupted his thoughts. "Still with me, son?"

"Uh, yeah. Sorry, Mom. Did you tell Riley?"

His mother softly touched his face. "Of course. Your sister sends her love."

He knew the answer before asking the question. "I'll be laid up for a while, won't I?"

"I'm afraid so."

As he expected. Sam tried to move his right leg, but something restrained it. *Another cast.* His heart sank and his mouth was suddenly dry. "Can I get something to drink?"

"Of course, baby." She grabbed a cup off a tray and offered him the straw.

The cool liquid inside felt refreshing when he swallowed. "They say how long I'll be stuck here?"

"The doctor said you can go home, maybe tomorrow or the day after. Oh, by the way, I met your friend Hannah last night. Ellie brought her over. The girl really wanted to see you. She's such a nice lady, but kinder and prettier than you told me. I liked her but more importantly, I can see why you like her."

Sam looked away. *Don't want to see her no more.* "How is she?"

"She told Harry she has a bad sprain. Hannah was in a wheelchair."

Sam winced. Hannah had been progressing nicely. He'd seen the pain on her face when Kyle twisted her arm. *Jerk, hurting Hannah like that.* "Glad to hear it's nothing more than a sprain. Look, Mom, can you call Riley again? I want to talk to her."

"Maybe in a little while. You need to rest."

He knew his mom wouldn't understand. "I want to stay with her, until I get better."

Rhonda's brows furrowed as she looked in Sam's eyes. "Why there? I don't mind taking care of you. After all, you *are* my baby."

"I know, but it'll be hard, with the four foster kids and stuff. They make a lot of racket. I'll need peace and quiet."

Rhonda shook her head. "You're not telling the truth. I can see right through you. What's wrong?"

Sam looked away. His mom would never understand. Just before he closed his eyes, he muttered, "Nothing."

***

Jake was exhausted. The tired and anguished face in the mirror was barely recognizable. The face of a man about to lose everything he really wanted. All of a sudden, determination swelled up from deep within him. No. This is incredibly stupid. *I will change my stars.* Last night, he'd had the Uber driver drop him in Ephrata. He'd spent the rest of the night walking the twelve miles or so back to his apartment in Witmer. Jake had wrestled the situation over in his mind before the light came on. And now he had a plan. *Screw Boston. Last night will not be the last time I see her. I would choose Daisy, every time.* Now he needed to make her understand how much he needed her. *And love her.*

Jake plugged his cell into the charger. It had run out of juice last night shortly after calling for a car.

From his closet, he grabbed khakis and a nice dress shirt. His throat tightened as he held the shirt that Daisy had given to him. *No, no, no!* His anger rose. Being a quitter wasn't in his spirit. *I won't let you go, Daisy.* His plan was a Hail Mary, he knew, but he refused to go down without a fight.

Joe Rohrer's face flashed before him. *I won't let you take her from me.* Doctor or not, Jake would confront the man. He would tell Rohrer that Jake needed Daisy. That he loved her. That any chance for his happiness rested in her arms. And then he would confess his love to Daisy.

Jake popped a pod of high test in the Keurig and headed to the shower. Despite the lack of sleep, he needed to be on the top of his game. *I'll be damned forever if I let you go, girl.* He turned the knob until the water steamed. The runaway train of fate was barreling down the track. Jake would meet it head on.

***

Daisy tried Jake's phone again, for maybe the hundredth time. Straight to voicemail. *Pick up, Jake, please.* She'd waited all her life for his return, so he would finally take notice. And last night, her happy future was within her grasp, but somehow, her dreams slipped through her fingers yet again.

She held her head in her hands. *Who am I kidding?* It was over. She'd read it in his eyes. As if to emphasize him not returning her calls, the finality of his words confirmed it. *"I'll never forget you."* As in, it's the last time you'll see me. Jake had made up his mind. He was heading to Boston, for his future. And a life that didn't include her.

Thank God her parents were away, so she didn't have to explain it to them. Daisy palmed her eyes and took another sip of the lukewarm tea. Memories flooded back. Of their first date at the Tea Room. Their magical time in Rehoboth. Long walks under the moonlight. Evenings spent holding hands along the Cocalico. *Why didn't I tell you I loved you when I had the chance?* So many wasted opportunities. She needed to tell him how she really felt. That she'd waited all these years for him to come back into her life. For Jake to love her in return. Now it's over. *Forever.*

Daisy spoke to her tea cup. "No way I'll survive today in the office." Not with everyone there, asking about her latest adventures with Mr. Right. But she couldn't take off. There was too much to do. "Maybe I can slip into the practice, grab my laptop and work from home." Yeah, that's what she'd do. She headed to her bedroom to put on some cosmetics to hide the hurt. *But no amount of makeup can cover my pain.*

Chapter 17

Hannah studied her image in the mirror. For the first time in ages, she actually looked pretty, despite those miserable crutches. Ellie had been wonderful, applying Hannah's makeup, and then styling her long, strawberry blonde hair into a bun. But what caught her attention was the sparkle in her own eyes. And that was there because she'd finally admitted what she felt in her heart for Sam. And that was love.

A voice rose inside her, tormenting her. *He's too young for you.* Okay, there was a twelve-year difference in age. She countered the voice of doubt. "We're closer in age than Dave and I were." Her husband had been twenty-five years older. *And how was your marriage to Dave? You always knew he was too old for you. Too old, like you are compared to Sam. How will that make Sam feel?* "I didn't have a choice." Hannah had been six months pregnant when Dave asked for her hand. His proposal was an escape. A father and name for a child that wasn't his.

Hannah adjusted the peach colored dress she'd borrowed from Ellie. *He was only a father figure, not a real husband.* No. Dave had been her husband, loving her, always caring more about her needs than his. *You tricked him into marrying you.* "No. I was honest with him. I told him what happened, as soon as he proposed. And he still married me." *He only treated you like he did to make up for the loss of his first wife.* Not true. Her husband had been so kind and compassionate, especially after she confessed what happened. "Dave always put me first. He... he loved me." Beth was almost two before they'd made love the first time.

Voices in the hallway drew her attention. Darcy and Ellie were talking. *What about Sam? Just a kid, isn't that what you said?* "I didn't mean it like that." *What can you offer him? Love, happiness? If he wants children, can you give him those at your age?* "I'll give him my heart. My soul. All my love. Everything I have. And yes, if Sam wants them, I'll have his babies."

The voices of doubt rose again. *Fool. When he's forty, you'll be fifty-two.* "There's a lot of living to share before I'm too old." *Do you think he'll love you forever? What happens when your age shows and he's still young?* Hannah slammed her hands against the dresser and screamed, "Shut up. Stop this!"

"I didn't say anything."

Hannah whipped around to see Ellie staring at her from the door.

Hannah's cheeks heated. "I'm sorry. I was having a disagreement with myself."

Ellie's eyes changed. "About what?"

"I, uh, it's not important."

Ellie covered the space between them and reached for Hannah's hands. "Yes, it is. You've been through a lot in the past day. I've been there, more times than I care to admit. Always seemed to be two voices. One was the voice of doubt and the second, my heart. I'll give you some advice, if I may. Always listen to your heart and follow what it tells you."

How can she know? Hannah hopped forward and wrapped her arms around Ellie. "You're such a great friend. Why are you being so kind to me?"

Ellie clung to her tightly. "God blessed us so richly. The passion that drives our business *and* our family is to help others. I think you need a hand, and a friend." Ellie pulled back and smiled, revealing a dimple on her chin and another on her cheek. "Besides, we like you."

Hannah's chest filled with gratitude. "You and I seem to have this, this connection. I feel it. Like you really know me."

The laughter from the other woman lifted Hannah's heart even more. "You remind me of someone, from when I was younger. And that someone was me. Kindness was shown and given to me, when I didn't deserve it. Now I'm paying back that debt." Ellie squeezed her hands. "You look beautiful today. Are you ready to go see Sam?"

Hannah's insides tingled and she nodded. "Yes." Her lips ached in anticipation of Sam's kiss.

***

Jake's fingers hurt. They were white from gripping the steering wheel so hard. *Where the hell is Rohrer?* The clock on the dash read eight forty-five. That meant he'd been outside the practice for an hour and a half. Waiting.

The white Camaro smoothly rolled into a space near the door on the far side of the building. Before Jake could move, Dr. Joseph Rohrer stepped out and disappeared into the back door. The man looked so confident, so sure of himself, so happy. *Of course he looks that way. He won Daisy's heart.*

Jake closed his eyes. "Please God, help me. Open his heart and let him see how much I love her. Please guide my actions and place the right words in my mouth. Amen." The metal door handle was cold and firm in his hand. He stepped out of his truck. The path to the double doors seemed miles long. He walked to the receptionist window.

Immediately, the girl behind the desk smiled, as if she knew a secret. "Good morning, Mr. Elliot. Daisy's not here yet. Is there something I can help you with?"

Jake could feel the perspiration forming on his brow. "Actually, I'm not here to see Daisy." *Yet.* "Is Dr. Rohrer available?"

The woman checked her computer screen. "His first patient's not due for another half hour. I'll see if he's available. Can I ask what this is about?"

Jake's words came out harsher than he meant. "No! I... uh, I mean, it's a personal matter." Murmurs started behind him. Other patients were talking. *About me.*

The smile left the receptionist's face and she pushed her chair back. "I'll go speak with him. Don't go anywhere."

Within a few seconds, Rohrer opened the door. Daisy's friend Trenton was standing behind him.

"Jake? Why don't you step into my office? Second door on your right. Come on in."

Jake walked into the room and took a seat. Rohrer slid into his chair, desk between them. Trenton stepped inside and closed the door. Rohrer studied Jake. "You seem agitated. Are you all right, Jake?"

Jake turned toward Trenton. "This is personal. Mind giving us a few minutes?"

Trenton shook his head. "Actually, I do."

Rohrer explained. "I asked him to step in with us because you scared the front desk girl. What's going on?"

"It's about Daisy."

The doctor stood. "Daisy? Is she all right? Did something happen to her?"

Jake's hands involuntarily flew in front of him. "No, no. She's fine." He again glanced at Trenton. "This is going to be hard enough without him here. Can we speak privately?"

Trenton answered. "Standard protocol for dealing with an agitated patient is to have two professionals in the room. I'm not leaving, until you do."

Jake felt his voice rise. "I'm not upset."

"Sure. And the Pope's not Catholic."

Rohrer cleared his throat. "Trenton, back it down a notch. How can I help you, Jake?"

"Daisy."

"What about her?"

"This, this can't happen. I won't let it."

The men exchanged a look of worry. "Won't let what happen? Explain yourself."

Jake's breath was hard to get out. He stood and walked to the window. The view outside was blurry. Trenton was there, mere inches away. "No easy way to say this." He turned to face the good doctor. "It's you. You're the one."

Rohrer looked puzzled. "The one? What do you mean?"

Jake palmed his eyes. "You're the guy she loves. Mr. Right, the man she wants to marry. I can't let that happen. I love Daisy. I need her. Don't you see? And I'm going to do everything I can to take her from you. I wanted to be man enough to let you know that in person."

Jake glanced at Trenton, and then at the doctor. To Jake's surprise, Rohrer struggled and tried to stifle back laughter. Trenton wasn't as restrained. He let out a loud guffaw and doubled over.

"What the hell's so funny? This is no laughing matter."

It took a few seconds before Rohrer could get control. "Daisy sent you here, didn't she? She loves to play practical jokes."

Jake's hands curled. "No, she didn't send me. And I didn't tell her I was coming. She said she was going to tell you today, that you're the one and she loves you."

The doctor's smile faded. "Did she say she was going to tell me, or she was going to tell Mr. Right?"

"Mr. Right—but that's you. I figured it out. The only man she spends any time with besides me is you. It has to be you." Jake felt the hot stream on his cheeks. He wiped it away with his arm.

Rohrer approached him. "Jake, you've got this all wrong. It is *definitely* not me. Isn't that right, Trenton?" Rohrer softly touched his arm.

Trenton patted Jake's other arm. "It isn't Joe Rohrer."

Jake slapped their hands away. "Yeah? Then tell me who it is."

Trenton slowly shook his head. "You really don't know? Man, you're a fool. How plain does she have to make it?"

Jake's anger was running away. He grabbed Trenton by the collar. "Then who is it?"

Trenton's eyes were full of anger as he shoved Jake away. "You really want to meet Mr. Right? Then come with me." Trenton opened the door and stepped into the hallway.

Jake saw nothing but red as he followed. "Introduce me to the low-life."

Trenton entered another room, Jake two steps behind him. Jake realized it was a restroom. "Why are we in here?"

The nurse manager grabbed Jake's chin and turned it so his reflection was in the mirror. "Jake Elliot, meet Daisy's Mr. Right."

***

Daisy slipped her Fusion into the spot next to the white Camaro. With any luck, she'd be in and out before anyone would know she'd been there. Quickly stepping inside the office, she ducked inside her room as Trenton exited Dr. Rohrer's office.

She heard Trenton talking. "Then come with me."

Every hair on her body stood on end when she heard a loud and angry voice. "Introduce me to the low-life." *Jake?*

Daisy strained to hear the conversation. A chill ran down her spine when Trenton spoke his next words. "Jake Elliot, meet Daisy's Mr. Right."

No, no. Not this way. Daisy stumbled into the corridor. Most of the staff was congregated in the walkway, trying to see the source of the angry voice.

Jake got even louder. "Me? What? How would you know that?"

Trenton's laugh rattled her to the core. "Everyone knows, except you, you stupid idiot. Every day she's been coming in, bragging about you and how perfect her Mr. Right is. Telling us about the exploits of her and Mr. Right."

The hall began to vibrate up and down. Jake was screaming. "So everyone knows? And I'm just the jerk caught in her web of lies. You were right, I am a fool. An idiot for believing she really cared."

Got to stop this. Daisy called out, "Jake, let me explain."

The man of her dreams stepped out and walked until he stood before her. "This was all some game to you, wasn't it?"

"No, Jake. You... you're the man I love."

"Really?" His voice mocked her. "You led me on. If you really cared, you would have told me. Instead, you made an ass of me while you and everyone here laughed behind my back."

"I did try to tell you, last night."

Jake's eyes had never been as wild as they were right now. "You little liar. Get away from me. I never want to see you again." He took another step toward her.

Rohrer was suddenly there. "Calm down now, Jake, or I'll call Security."

Jake shoved him harshly against the wall.

"That's enough. You're out of here!" Trenton grabbed Jake's arm and twisted it violently behind his back. "Don't you dare talk to my friend like that, ever!" Trenton forced Jake down the hall. "Open the back door." Daisy chanced a glance. One of the nurses wrenched the portal open and Trenton threw him outside. "Leave. You come back in here again and I'll call the police."

Let this be a bad dream. Joe was at her side. "Are you okay?"

Everything was spinning. "No, I'm feeling dizzy." Rohrer swept her in his arms just before everything turned black.

Chapter 18

H enry Campbell walked from the office toward the home he shared with Ellie. As he passed the employee parking lot, a rustling noise captured his attention. The wind was blowing a paper stuck between the windshield and the wiper on a car. Hannah Rutledge's car. Curiosity got the better of him. Henry walked over and removed the slip. His blood ran cold when he read the words.

This ain't over. You and them Campbells plotted to get me fired, huh? Let me tell you, payback's a bitch. You and them better watch your backs.

Henry folded the paper and stuck it in his pocket. He pulled his cell and fired off a text to Ellie.

Have to run an errand. Won't be too long. I love you.

He retraced his steps into the office and opened Kyle's personnel file. Henry memorized the address and walked to his truck. In less than twenty minutes, he stood in front of a weathered apartment door in Christiana. Henry knocked several times before a man he'd never seen opened the door.

"What do you want?"

"Is Kyle in?"

"Who wants to know?" In no mood for the jerk's cocky attitude, Henry shoved him aside and entered the apartment. There was Kyle, seated on a filthy couch along with three other unsavory men.

Kyle sneered. "Unless you came here to beg me to come back to your stupid job, hit the pike, you limey."

Henry smiled. "Hello to you, too, Kyle. Was that meant as a compliment or an insult? You know, I did serve her Majesty. Six years in the Royal Marines. And damned proud of it. Or were you trying to insult me because I'm Scottish?"

"Get out."

"I will, then. But first, you and I need to talk. About the note you left for Hannah."

"Didn't leave no note on her car. Can't prove nothin'."

Henry nodded. "I didn't say where I found it, but your words are proof enough for me. Want to discuss this matter in front of your friends or one on one?"

Kyle nodded to the other men. They stood and surrounded Henry on all sides. "Leave or we'll kick the crap out of you."

Henry took off his coat and dropped it to the floor. "Try and make me leave. I dare ya. All of you little lassies."

One of Kyle's friends lunged. Henry dealt with him quickly. In thirty seconds, all four of Kyle's buddies were unconscious on the floor. Kyle tried to back away, but Henry grabbed his hand, twisting it viciously until Kyle was on his knees.

"Hmm. Now where were we?"

"Stop! That hurts. Didn't mean no harm. I was just funnin'."

"You threatened my family, and Hannah."

"I was just kidding!"

Henry twisted Kyle's arm until the man was face down on the carpet, Henry's boot firmly against the younger man's neck. "I'll only say this once, so pay close attention. You listening?" Henry yanked the arm tighter.

"Yes! Yes!"

"Good. If I ever see you anywhere near my family, you'll deal with me and I won't be as pleasant."

"Okay."

"And if you hurt any of them, I will break every bone in your body. One at a time and very slowly."

"All right. I get it. Don't hurt me no more."

Henry released Kyle's arm and used his foot to turn the man onto his back. "Same goes for Hannah and her girls. Mess with them and there will be hell to pay. And I'll be the one collecting. You understand?"

"Yeah."

Henry kicked his ribs. "Yeah, what?"

"Yes, sir."

Henry grabbed Kyle by the throat and yanked him from the floor until they were nose to nose. "I never want to have this conversation again. Understand me?"

Kyle nodded because Henry's grip closed the man's airway. Henry released him after Kyle passed out.

Henry turned as he stood in the doorway. "I pray for your sake you got the message. Next time, I won't play nice." The whoosh of the slamming door shook the entire wall.

***

Sam sucked on the straw from the cup his mother offered. She wiped his mouth with a napkin. "Mom, you don't have to stay here and treat me like a baby. You've got the kids to care for."

"Son, no one's as important to me as you are right now. Let's talk this over again. Please explain why you insist on going to Riley's place."

"Because it will be loud at home. I want to be somewhere quiet. I need time to think."

His mother brushed his hair from his eyes. "Think about what?"

Sam shook his head to get her hand off of him. "My future."

Rhonda smiled. "I think we both know your future is here. In Lancaster. Strasburg to be specific, where Hannah and her girls live."

"No, not no more."

"Why would you even say that?"

"Because."

"Because of what?"

"Mom..."

"I raised a son who always told the truth. Taught him never to hold anything back. You know our family is built on honesty. Do I need to ask again?"

Sam's nose itched. He tried to scratch, but the bandage over the bridge made it difficult. "Mom, please stop."

"I will. As soon as you answer my question, truthfully."

His eyes were scratchy. "Hannah."

To his surprise, another woman's voice answered. "Yes?"

His eyes turned to the two women standing at the door, Ellie Campbell and Hannah. Hannah was wearing a peach colored dress. Despite supporting herself on crutches, she looked exquisite. He'd never seen a more beautiful sight. She hobbled over. Rhonda moved the chair so Hannah could sit down.

Hannah grasped his hand. "Oh Sam, you poor guy. Does your nose hurt? What about your eyes? I was so worried about you. Great to see you awake." She quickly wiped her free hand across her cheeks. "I was so scared. Thank you... for everything yesterday. For coming to my rescue, for..."

Sam cut her off. "Sorry, Hannah. I don't feel like visitors right now. I need a nap."

Her face paled and she released his hand. "Okay. Should I stop by later?"

Sam caught the questioning look between Rhonda and Ellie. "No need to do that. You're hurt, too. Go home. Don't mean to be rude, but I'm... I'm just exhausted. The meds, you know." He forced himself to yawn, then closed his eyes and pretended to fall asleep.

After a few seconds of silence, he heard Hannah whisper, "Maybe this was a mistake, me coming here."

Rhonda's voice was calming. "Nonsense. My boy, he's been through a lot. That's all."

A sniffle came to his ears. *Please don't cry, Hannah.* "Because of me. It's all my fault," he heard her say.

Then he heard footsteps. His mother answered, "No, it's not. Things, they just happen sometimes."

Ellie chimed in, "I'm glad Sam was there when Kyle assaulted you. Did the police come talk to Sam yet? Henry decided to press charges against that brute."

Rhonda's voice was quiet. "No, not yet."

"Kyle needs to pay for what he did. Henry fired him, but we're still concerned, for Hannah. Kyle has anger issues. Henry thinks a little time in jail might make Kyle think differently."

The room grew quiet, but Sam could detect soft whispers. He was curious, and it took all of his resolve not to peek.

He heard Ellie's voice next. "When's the last time you ate, Rhonda?"

"Yesterday. I didn't want to leave Sam by himself."

You could have.

Hannah spoke up. "I can stay with him while you get something."

No. Don't make it any harder. Just leave.

Ellie countered. "Let him rest. Why don't we head to the cafeteria? All three of us. We'll drop by afterwards. Maybe he'll feel like a visit then."

Hannah again. "Are you sure, I mean, do you think he'll be okay? Suppose he needs something? I don't mind waiting here."

Rhonda entered the conversation. "The call light is right by his side. The nursing staff seems pretty helpful. He'll be fine. And besides, maybe I can get to know you a little bit. In case you didn't know, my son likes you. A whole lot."

Mother! Sam felt his cheeks heat. Lips brushed against his head. His mom's. "Love you, Sammy. Sweet dreams."

The sound of a chair being pushed back was followed by other creaking noises. Hannah's crutches. Soon, the only sounds were the ones from the hallway. Still, Sam counted to a hundred before opening his eyes. The first thing he saw was Hannah's face, chin resting on the bed rail, mere inches from his.

Her lips were smiling. "I knew you were playing possum."

***

The irritating odor of ammonia tore through Daisy's olfactory senses. A quick glance revealed she was on an examination table in one of the patient rooms. She tried to sit up, but hands were restraining her. Those hands belonged to Trenton, her *ex*-friend.

"Easy, Daze, easy. You passed out."

Joe Rohrer was also there. He used his flashlight to check her eyes. "How are you feeling, Daisy?"

She shoved Trenton's arms away. "Get your paws off of me! This is all your fault."

Daisy sat up and swung her legs over the side. That was a mistake, because she lost her balance and started to fall. Dr. Rohrer again grabbed her and gently lifted her back onto the table. "Daisy, calm down. Let's take this nice and slow."

Her cheeks and nose were wet. *Jake.* "I need to talk to him, now. Make him understand."

Trenton raised his voice. "No. The man is a flaming idiot, with a temper to boot. I'm just glad we were there. Who knows what he would have done to you?"

The anger flowing through her body reached her mouth. "The only thing flaming in this room is you. You did this! It is all your fault. You made him mad. Why in the world did you tell him that?"

"Tell him what? That he was Mr. Right? Because he was too stupid to realize it himself. He's like a dull crayon. Someone had to break the news to him."

"Yes! Me! I should have been the one to tell him, not you."

"I did you a favor. Forget him, Daisy. Even on his best day, he was never worthy of you."

Daisy hauled her arm back and slapped Trenton. Rohrer wrapped his arms around her. "That's enough. No more, Daisy. It'll be fine, you'll see."

She struggled in the doctor's arms. "Yeah, right. I've lost him for good, thanks to your big mouth, Trenton."

Her friend was rubbing his cheek. "You'll thank me some day. I did you a favor."

Joe snapped. "Just shut up. You're not helping the situation. Why don't you give Daisy a little space?"

Trenton's lips drew together into a thin white line. "Fine. When you come to your senses, I'll still be here. Don't forget... *I'm* your friend."

Daisy's breath was coming in rasps. "If that's how you show friendship, then you're an idiot and I don't want to be your friend anymore. You stay away from me, you hear?"

"Fine!" Trenton left, slamming the door behind him.

The doctor held her hand. "Try to breathe slowly. Everything will be okay."

"Sure it will. The man I've loved forever just told me he never wants to see me again."

Joe sighed. "Jake didn't mean what he said." He grew quiet. "Daisy, do you know why he came here today?"

Her chin was quivering. "N-no."

"He thought I was the one you wanted. That I was Mr. Right. Jake told me he loved you and needed you. He came to tell me he was going to do everything in his power to take you away from me."

Daisy shook her head violently. "You never had me. My heart has always belonged to him."

"*You* know that... and so do I. But Jake didn't. And when Trenton told him that everyone here knew—that you were always bragging him up—Jake misunderstood. That's why he got upset. I imagine he thought you were making fun of him."

"But I wasn't."

Joe took his fingers and pushed her hair from her eyes. "We both understand that, too. Just let him cool down. I'm sure he'll come to his senses."

She sniffed. "How can you be so sure?"

Nothing but understanding was in his eyes. "You weren't there. You didn't see the emotion in his face. The man loves you like crazy."

"Then why did he act like that?"

"It's hard to explain, but he's a man."

Daisy's head snapped to engage his eyes. "And what exactly does that mean? It's a poor excuse."

Joe sighed. "You're right, it is. You have to understand, we men are prideful creatures. We're not like women. This will sound strange, but girls are more logical, less emotional when it comes to matters of the heart. Men don't know how to express our feelings, so we overreact. Sometimes."

"Are all men like that? Is that how you would have acted?"

"To be honest, probably yes. If I was in Jake's shoes, I'd have been hurt. But there's a good point in all of this."

Daisy shook her head. "I don't how any good could come out of today."

He patted her hand. "There is. You see, I think I know your man fairly well. After he calms down, Trenton's words will sink in."

"Which ones? That I made a fool of him?"

"No." Joe touched the side of her face, raising her chin so they were eye to eye. "That you love him."

Daisy sobbed before answering. "God, I hope so."

Chapter 19

T he whispered conversation had been because the women knew Sam was only pretending to be asleep. The blush on his face when Rhonda said he liked Hannah, a lot, had given away his ploy.

Open your eyes, Sam.

His lips had moved as he counted. It took all Hannah had not to break out in laughter. The shock when he finally opened his eyes was even more proof.

Hannah couldn't help but smile. "I knew you were playing possum."

Sam moved as far from her as possible. "Wasn't pretending. I w-was asleep. You woke me."

"Sure I did. Okay, sorry. We're finally alone." Hannah felt her smile dissipate as she watched his eyes. *Fear?* Of what? "What's wrong?"

"I've got a bad headache. Kyle really worked me over."

"I'm sorry. Does your nose hurt?"

"Of course it does. He broke it."

Hannah gently took his hand. He quickly pulled free from her grasp. "Don't you want me to be here?"

His lips were set firmly. "Not really."

What? "Sam, I've been waiting to see you since this happened. I was concerned about my best friend."

He closed his eyes tightly and looked away. "Stop saying that."

"Why? You know it's true." A chill ran down her spine. "Are you upset because this happened? I get the feeling you're angry with me and I don't know why. Can you talk to me?"

Sam reclined his head and concentrated on the ceiling. "Talk about what?"

"Why are you angry with me?"

"I'm not."

Hannah shook her head. "I know you too well, Samuel Espenshade. You're angry. At me."

He spewed his response. "Do not call me Samuel. I hate that name."

"Sorry, Sam. What's wrong, honey?"

"I'm pissed."

"At me?"

"No, at *him*. Kyle knew about my leg. He broke it, in the same place it was broken before."

Hannah softly touched his face. "Your mom said you were in a car accident. What happened?"

Sam's eyes were suddenly red. "I don't want to talk about it."

"But I need to know. As time goes on, I want to know everything."

He shook his head and bit his lips. "It's too hard. I don't want to relive it again. Worst day of my life."

"But your mom said..."

"She talks too much. Look, I mean no disrespect, but leave me alone. I'm having a hard enough time

164

going through this again, without you pressing the issue."

"Honey, I'm only trying to help. Please don't feel..."

"And quit calling me honey. I'm *only* your friend, nothing else."

It was as if someone had slapped her. *Is this all in my mind?* "I don't understand."

Sam was now visibly fighting not to sob. "Leave me alone. Please?" He turned his head from her.

It was all Hannah could do to not cry. "Is that what you really want?"

"Y-yes. Be gone. Let me alone."

"Hey, guys. I see my son is awake."

Hannah turned to see Ellie and Rhonda standing behind her, smiles on their faces. Their expressions quickly faded when they noted the look on Hannah's face.

"What's going on?" Rhonda asked.

Sam's voice was high-pitched. "I want to be by myself. Please everyone, get out of here."

Hannah turned to Ellie. "Can I have my crutches? I'd like to go now."

"Sure." Ellie walked out, returning with those dreaded metal instruments.

Hannah hoisted herself up, turning for one last look at Sam. "If you're angry at me, I'm sorry, but I really don't understand why. Something's going on in your mind and I wish you'd let me in. You're my best friend and I need you. I'd like to think you need me, too. When you're ready, tell me. I'll always be here for you." Then she grabbed his hand and kissed it but he quickly pulled free.

"Goodbye, Hannah." Sam covered his eyes with his hands.

"Goodbye, Sam." *What did I do?* She would ponder that for many a night.

***

Despite everything she tried, Ellie didn't seem to be able to comfort Hannah. Her friend was laying aimlessly on the couch, staring at the television. The knock on the door seemed to be a reprieve.

Ellie opened the door to find a police officer standing there, soaked from the downpour. "May I help you?" she asked.

The officer tipped his hat, rain running off the brim. "Evening, ma'am. I'm looking for Henry Campbell. Is he here?"

He must be here about the charges Henry filed. "Of course. Please come in from the rain. Follow me into the dining room and I'll get Henry."

After the man was seated, Ellie scampered upstairs to the room she shared with her husband. He was on the bed, reading a book while their daughter slept next to him. "Henry? A police officer is here. He asked to speak with you."

Ellie could see as well as feel his anger. "About time." She was confused when he grabbed a paper from a drawer. "Ask Mum to keep an eye on Maggie. I want you to be there, to hear about this." He held the paper between his fingers.

After getting her mother-in-law to watch their daughter, Ellie entered the dining room. She could tell right away something was dreadfully wrong.

The officer's tone was not pleasant. "You do realize I could charge you with making terroristic threats and five counts of assault, don't you?"

Henry's voice was full of anger. "Did you not hear what I read to you? Kyle threatened my family and Hannah."

"It's only circumstantial right now that he was the one who wrote this. Hand the note to me. It's evidence in the investigation."

Ellie was shaking inside as Henry threw the paper. "Here. Take your precious paper. No matter what you say, I have a right to protect my family."

Ellie grabbed the note and read it. "Oh my God."

The officer shook his head and took the paper from Ellie. "Mr. Campbell, you should have contacted the police immediately and not taken matters into your own hands."

"No disrespect, but I will protect my family at all costs. I wanted to make that perfectly clear to him."

"You beat those five men senseless. I can arrest you... right now."

Henry bolted to his feet. The veins on his head stood out. "They attacked me. Five against one and because I won, you're threatening to arrest me?"

The officer stood, taking a defensive posture. "Let me ask you this, Mr. Campbell. I heard you were a former Royal Marine. A Commando in the Royal Navy. Is that true?"

"Of course."

The officer shook his head. "The court will only hold that against you. They will look at your skills and training. And they will hold you accountable, whether they attacked first or not."

Ellie could feel her husband's anger. She touched Henry's arm. "You got into a fight?"

Henry flinched under her fingers. "I went to talk to Kyle. To warn him to stay away from you. I made my feelings crystal clear."

Ellie's world was crumbling. *Henry could go to prison.* "Officer, there's got to be something we can do. Should I call a lawyer?"

The officer took a deep breath. "There is one thing that could make all this go away."

She knew Henry's anger wouldn't allow him to speak sensibly. "What is that?"

"Drop your charges against Mr. Parker. He indicated if you drop yours, he'll withdraw his."

Henry's fists were shaking. "And let him get away with what he did to Sam, and Hannah?"

The officer removed a set of handcuffs from his belt. "Unfortunately, yes. You need to decide right now. If you don't drop the charges, I need to place you under arrest."

Henry stuck his hands in front of him. "Then do it."

The officer shook his head a third time and slapped the cuffs on Henry's right wrist.

Ellie screamed, "No, no! We'll drop them."

Her husband turned to her. "Eleanor..."

Her voice was high. "Your daughter is upstairs on our bed. If they arrest you, what will happen? Do you want me to raise her by myself? Please, Henry. Forget about it."

Henry was breathing harshly as he studied his wife. She felt him calm as he closed his eyes. "I'll do it for you, and Maggie, but not for me." He turned to the policeman. "I rescind the charges."

The officer removed the cuffs. "I think you made the right choice, Mr. Campbell, under the circumstances. You might not have seen your family for a long, long time. Next time, leave matters like this to the authorities." He tipped his hat to Ellie. "'Night, ma'am."

Henry closed the door behind the policeman. His anger and sorrow were coming in loud and clear. "Sorry, Ellie."

She wrapped her arms around him. "I understand what you did, but please, never do anything that stupid again. Please? Promise me."

Henry kissed her hair. "I promise, on our love."

Chapter 20

F our days had passed since Hannah's visit with Sam. She missed him so much, but he'd made it clear he didn't want company... or was it just *her* company? *What are you going through?* Whatever it was, Hannah was prepared to help him, in any and every way she could. He was too important just to forget.

Outside, the late October sun cast a yellow haze over the landscape. It was Monday afternoon. While Missi napped, Hannah finished mixing the special icing for the cake she'd baked earlier, as a way to repay Ellie and her family for their kindness. Henry had insisted she stay at their home. *Home?* No, this house was more than a home. It might look like a mansion, yet it was filled with something else. Something special. Love. And the love this family exuded made her dream thoughts she hadn't yet told anyone about.

Darcy Campbell walked into the kitchen, with little Maggie May on her hip. Hannah smiled. Darcy was quickly becoming the mother Hannah never had. Her birth mother had dropped Hannah off at her Aunt Mary's house for a weekend when Hannah was six. But that mother never came back. Ever. Her aunt had griped, complained and taken it out on that little girl every day she stayed there.

"I swear. This wee one is always hungry. Surprised she doesn't weigh fifty pounds." Darcy glanced at the cake pan. "That looks tasty. What kind did you make?"

Hannah smiled at the compliment from the master chef. "Spice cake infused with coconut milk. I'm making triple chocolate icing, with white chocolate drizzle and maraschino cherries on top." *Sam's favorite.* "Maybe Ellie will give me a lift to the hospital tonight. I'd like to take a slice to Sam."

Darcy stared at her strangely. "I thought Ellie said he'd been discharged two days ago."

The hair on the back of Hannah's neck stood up. "I, uh, I didn't know that."

Darcy's face turned red. "Maybe I wasn't supposed to say anything."

Hannah set the spreading knife on the counter and looked at the older woman. "You weren't supposed to tell me? Why not?"

Relief could be seen on Darcy's face when a knock sounded on the door. "Excuse me. Got to see who's here."

Hannah shivered, despite the warmth of the kitchen. *Why wouldn't they tell me?*

"Hi, Hannah." Hannah turned to see Rhonda, Sam's mother, standing across the counter. "What a heavenly scent. Sam always brags about your baking."

The chill increased as Hannah studied Rhonda's reaction. Sam's mom looked sad. "It's almost finished. Want a slice?"

"Maybe later. Can we sit and talk for a few minutes? I asked Darcy to give us some privacy." Rhonda pulled out one of the kitchen stools and patted her hand on it. Hannah limped over. Rhonda sat next to her and took her hands.

An unexplainable panic filled her heart. Hannah's hands shook in Rhonda's grip. "Why am I getting the feeling this isn't going to be a pleasant conversation?"

Rhonda touched her face. "Never was good at hiding things. I wear my feelings on my sleeve. Just like you do, Hannah. Just like you." Sam's mother grimaced. Her voice was low when she spoke again. "I need your help."

"My help? I don't understand."

"Let's get right to the point. You can't hide the fact, Hannah. You're in love with my son."

Hannah's mouth went dry. "I, uh, you could say... Wait. How could you possibly know? We've only just met."

Rhonda winked. "I could tell the second I met you. The thing you wanted to tell Sam when we were waiting for him to get out of surgery was that you loved him, wasn't it?"

The chill disappeared as heat flushed her face. *Who is this woman?* Hannah squeezed her eyes tightly. As much as she wanted to, Hannah couldn't lie. Her voice was barely a whisper. "Yes."

"It's okay, Hannah. I know my son. Sam's in love with you, too."

Relief and warmth trickled down her arms. *Then it isn't just me?* Just as quickly, coldness again wrapped icy arms around her. "But, there's more, isn't it? W-w-why doesn't he want to see me?"

Rhonda's eyes seemed to cloud. "Has he told you about the accident?"

"I was there."

"I'm not talking about this one. The accident that happened two years ago."

It was difficult to get her breath. "No."

Rhonda's cheeks were suddenly wet. "Sam was in a horrible car wreck. Coming home from Ohio. Jenna was driving, bringing him back. On the Pennsylvania Turnpike, east of Breezewood, a deer ran out in front of them." Rhonda walked to the window briefly before returning to sit down next to Hannah. "Jenna swerved to miss the animal. But she lost control. Her car ran off the road and rolled into a deep ravine." Sam's mother extracted a tissue from her pocket and dabbed her eyes. "Sam was pinned and his leg was crushed. Couldn't get free. His cell was in the back, out of reach. He was trapped."

Hannah squeezed Rhonda's hand, tightly. "Who was Jenna? His girlfriend?"

Rhonda choked back a sob. "No. Jenna was my youngest daughter... Sam's sister."

Hannah's heart seemed to stop. "Was? Is she okay?"

The older woman shook her head and wiped her eyes. "It was almost two days before the State Police found the wreck. Jenna's seatbelt nicked the artery in her neck. Sam tried to save her, but couldn't. She bled out. Died in her brother's arms."

Hannah gasped. *Poor Sam.* "Oh Rhonda, I'm so sorry."

Sam's mother grabbed her tissue again and blew her nose. "God must have needed my little girl more than I did. At least she didn't die alone."

"I can't even imagine... Must have been so hard on you."

"It was a horrible time. I almost lost my son, too."

"From his leg wounds?"

Rhonda sniffed hard. From somewhere in the house, the baby was crying. "No. Having Jenna die in his arms, being soaked in her blood and then not being able to get away from her dead body... for almost two days. It nearly cost Sam his sanity."

Little Maggie's screaming cries got louder. Darcy peeked in. "Sorry to interrupt. Can I grab another bottle from the fridge? This child's a bottomless pit."

Rhonda's smile was kind. "Sure. We don't mind."

Hannah caught the errant tear slowly tracking down Sam's mother's cheek.

After Darcy departed, Rhonda turned to her again. "Do you know when Sam finally came out of his funk? When he returned to normal?"

An eerie feeling touched Hannah's shoulders. "No. When?"

Rhonda's eyes were intense. "When *you* came into his life. You gave him joy, and hope. For the first time in a long time, he had a real purpose to live."

Hannah's mouth was dry. "I, uh, I never..."

"But now, my Sam is back in that same, desolate valley again. Waking up in the hospital took him back to those horrible days after Jenna's death. He's hurting so badly. Thank God something's different now."

"Different? What's that?"

"You. I really believe, girl, you are the key to making him whole again."

Hannah didn't know what to say or think. "I'll help him any way I can. What can I do?"

Rhonda engulfed her in her arms. "Be yourself. He's in a terrible place. That's why he went to Cleveland, to get away from here."

What? Hannah pulled away to look at Rhonda's face. "Cleveland? Why would he go there?"

"To escape the nightmare. To think what his future might hold and also to be with his other sister, Riley."

Hannah had to steady herself on the stool. *He moved away?* "How can I help him, if he's out there?"

Rhonda held her head. "That's why I'm here. I'm hoping together you and I can come up with a plan."

Hannah listened intently to Rhonda's idea. It would mean Hannah would need to leave her comfort zone. To take a chance. To help this man she loved. Fear filled her heart, yet another voice comforted her. But fear again raised its ugly head. *Can I even do this?*

***

Sam repositioned himself on the couch. His leg itched, something fierce. But the sensation was inside the cast, so he'd just have to suffer. *Go figure.*

Riley entered the room. She wore a solid red dress. She didn't have makeup on, but Sam didn't think his sister needed it. She'd always been the pretty one in the family. Besides, the studio would apply the final touches before she stepped in front of the camera.

Riley pinched his cheek. "You're up early. Big plans?"

It was three in the morning. Sam grunted. "Couldn't sleep. Plan on watching *Star Wars* on Netflix."

"Yeah? Which episode?"

"All of them."

Riley disappeared into her kitchenette, returning with a bowl of cereal and some juice for her brother. "How are you feeling this morning?"

"Miserable."

"Want some pain medicine?"

"No."

She shook her head. "You rest up today. This afternoon, we'll play some board games."

"Excitement at its finest. Look, you don't need to baby me. I could have stayed home and let Mom do that."

Riley sat next to him. "You came here for a reason. To get away from those memories. This is your safe place, but we need to start thinking about what's next. I won't let you hide from your life forever. Next week, you have an appointment with the doctor. I want you to ask him about rehabilitation."

Sam shook his head. "Riley..."

She glanced at her watch and then stood. "I've got to hit the road. Think about what I said. If you don't mention it to the doctor, I will." She touched his face. "I just care, that's all. Gotta go. Bye, Scooter."

With a peck on his forehead, she was gone. *I hate that name.*

Sam turned on the station where his sister worked, but his mind wasn't on the TV. He never told Riley, but he watched her station whenever she was working. While he waited for his sibling to come on, Sam's mind drifted. To Hannah and the futility of it all.

In his mind, he was talking to her. *"I tried everything I could to be your friend, to make you notice me. I was in love with you. And just when I thought you really cared... What did you say? That I'm just a kid. Don't you know how I feel, or don't you care?"*

The early edition of the news flashed on the screen, but Sam really didn't notice. All his bleary vision saw was Hannah's green eyes and her beautiful face.

Chapter 21

D aisy sat, watching the snow flurries tease the bare winter ground. *Dreary outside, just like my future.* It was barely a week until the holiday. They were predicting a white Christmas. *My last one here.* She took a sip of the orange spiced tea.

"I don't think you've said two words to me. Maybe we shouldn't have come to the Tea Room. I hoped it might cheer you up."

Daisy turned, catching the disappointment on her mother Vivian's face. "Sorry, Mom."

The older woman sighed. "Penny for your thoughts."

"I don't think you'll want to hear what I'm thinking."

Vivian reached across and touched her daughter's hand. "Of course I do."

Daisy sniffed. *This is going to be hard on Mom.* Daisy concentrated on the tea in her cup. "I can't stay here anymore. I think it's t-t-time I set out on my own."

Her mother's eyes widened. "Just out of the house, or away from Lancaster?"

Daisy turned to face Vivian. "Everywhere I go, all I think about is Jake. I hear his voice, I see his smile. I can feel him all around me. Memories of our time together haunt me, Mom. And people at work whisper behind my back. I know they're talking about me... and *him*."

Vivian frowned. "Maybe it's time to let Jake go. You know, there are other young men out there. Good men. That doctor you work with, for example. The one who's always so kind. What was his name again?"

"Rohrer. Joe Rohrer."

"Yes, that one. You always say how he treats you with respect."

"Mom..."

"He's so nice. Why don't the two of you go out? I bet that..."

"Stop it. I love Jake. If I can't have him, I don't want anyone else."

Vivian was quiet. "Did you try to call Jake?"

Daisy wiped her cheeks. "Every day. He sent me a text last week, telling me to leave him alone, not to contact him anymore. Said he was blocking my number and he won't return my texts from now on."

The hostess came over and dropped off two more teapots. "I wonder what happened to Ashley. And Sophie. Haven't seen them lately." Daisy had really enjoyed the company of those two.

Her mother ignored the chance to change the subject. "I don't know. But I believe it's time to move on. Let's come up with a plan."

Daisy's lips were set. "I have, Mom. I applied for a job, managing a small tourist airplane company."

Her mother's face turned pale. "What? Where?"

"Hawaii. Hilo to be exact. On the big island."

Vivian grew silent. Daisy glanced at her mother. The older woman's eyes were wet and she shook her head. "Is that what you really want?"

No, I want to marry Jake. "I think moving to Hawaii would be best. Gives me a chance to start over. Somewhere new, where memories of Jake won't preoccupy me."

"But Daisy, I need you. Here."

Daisy held her mother's trembling hand. "I need you, too, but I have to do this. For me. As a way to keep my sanity."

"You're being impulsive. Why move away? You've lived in the same house for thirty-one years."

Please understand. "And thank you for that. For allowing me to live at home. For being my rock, my best friend. But we both know, it's time I struck out on my own."

Her mother wiped a hand across her face. "If that's what you want to do, then, I-I'll support you on this."

Daisy shook her head. "It's not what I want to do. It's what I need to do."

***

"Hey, bro. Can I make you something before I leave?"

Sam re-directed his gaze from the television to his sister, Riley. "No. I'll scrounge up something later, when I'm ready to pass out from hunger. What about you?"

"Didi and I'll grab something at the game." Didi was the traffic girl who worked with his sister. She and Riley were tight. *Very pretty, by the way.* Much to Sam's extreme pleasure, Didi had been a frequent visitor at the apartment since Sam arrived.

Ignoring the previous conversation, Riley brought over a plate of re-heated pizza. She studied his eyes. "Here. Despite you eating me out of house and home, I'd never forgive myself if you died from hunger. Glad to see you're up and moving. I was really worried about you when you got here."

A deep sigh left Sam. "Thanks for letting me crash with you. Hopefully I'm not cramping your style too much."

"Well, I did have to cancel the Thursday night raves and the Saturday afternoon poker tournaments..."

He nodded his head. "You're the best. I really appreciate that we can talk so openly. There's just some things I can't talk to Mom about."

Riley sat next to him. "Oh, you mean Hannah?" Sam nodded. "Your secret's safe. Mom thinks you're torn up about Jenna, that waking up in the hospital brought back bad memories."

"Yeah, it did, but I've come to terms with that. But the whole deal with Hannah..." Sam shook his head. "Broke my heart, what she said."

His big sister patted his hand. "From what you told me, I wouldn't be so hard on her. After all, she wasn't having an in-depth conversation about her love life with her attacker." She brushed his hair from his eyes. "Try putting yourself in her shoes. I know you love her and from what Mom says, Hannah cares about you, too. A lot... maybe even *love*. Perhaps it's time you two had a heart to heart."

Sam shook his head. "No matter how she meant it, it's true. I'm just a kid. I should be with someone my own age and she should be with someone older."

The devilish smile on Riley's face warned him that teasing was next. "Didi has a crush on you. She's only twenty-two, and gorgeous to boot. A real nice *kid*." Her smile eased. "Just like my brother. I could set you up."

"I'm not going to hit on your best friend."

She smacked his arm. "She's not my best friend. You are, you big lug."

His sight was suddenly blurred as he thought of *both* his sisters. "Such a lucky guy, having you as my sister." Sam decided to tease back. "But if you want to set me up, how about Miana, your weather girl? Talk about hot..."

"Miana? She's thirty and besides, she's not really into guys."

"Ooh, a challenge. Maybe introducing her to someone as handsome as me might make a difference."

Riley stood and brushed his head with her lips. "Now that's my brother. Always thinking more of himself than anyone else does. You have a great evening. See you after the game."

After Riley left, Sam re-positioned on the sofa. He selected another movie from Netflix—*Raiders of the Lost Ark*. While he'd watched this Indiana Jones film several times over the past week, there was nothing else to do. Riley was on her assignment at a Cavaliers basketball game. It was so lonely staying here by himself.

The ringing of his cell phone caught his attention. He glanced at the number and didn't recognize it. The call was from a 717 area code. Southcentral Pennsylvania. Probably just another telemarketer. *At least it will be someone to talk to.* He depressed the accept button. "Hello?" His mouth went dry when he recognized the voice.

***

Hannah took a deep breath before calling. Her hands were shaky. She'd forced herself to buy the cell phone. Dale Olphin's threats still haunted her mind. *My brother can track you down, no matter where you are.* Dale's brother was the county sheriff. When she left Oklahoma, she'd done her best to limit her profile, paying cash for everything. Making sure there was very little that was traceable. When she needed money, she drove to Baltimore to draw cash from her accounts, but never from the same bank or branch. She didn't want to risk her new life.

But getting a phone was something she had to do. The void left by Sam's absence was horrible. She missed her best friend. *It's now or never.* Beth was visiting with her friend, Selena. Missi was at a play date with another toddler. *I need to hear his voice.*

She dialed the number Rhonda had provided. Sam's cell number. It rang once, then twice. Her tense body relaxed when he answered. "Hello?"

Another deep breath. "Hi, Sam. Remember me?"

There was a long pause before he spoke. "Hannah? Oh my gosh! Hannah, is that really you?"

"The one and only. I missed you, so much. How've you been?"

Despite the distance, she could sense his astonishment. "I-I thought you didn't like to talk on the phone."

"I never said that. I just didn't have one. But I just got an iPhone, and guess who the first person I called was? You. Tell me you're doing okay."

"Yeah, I'm great, er, uh, I mean..." Sam faked a cough. "A little under the weather. Trying to catch up on my sleep."

Hannah smiled. He was lying, she knew, but the sound of his voice was such a comfort. "I see. I won't keep you long."

"Uh, well, I'm up now. How about you? Your ankle okay?"

So he did think of me. At least a little. "It's coming slow. I'm able to put weight on it again. Painful, but at least the crutches are history. I hate those blamed things."

Sam snorted. "Yeah, I agree. I've got about three months to go before I get rid of mine." He grew quiet. "How are you, really? And your girls? I hope Beth's helping out a lot."

"I don't know if you remember, but Henry and Ellie took us in. I think it was partially because of Kyle. You were right. The Campbells are such a nice family."

"Sure are. Helped me when I needed it."

An opening. A chance to get him to talk about dealing with the loss of Jenna. To help his mind. "When did you need their help?"

The voice on the phone was momentarily silent. "Not important. How's Harry?"

Hannah frowned. "Not quite sure. Harry must have gone away for a while. And oh, I forgot to tell you. His brother Edmund had an accident. Broke his right arm, pretty badly. Had surgery to pin it back together."

"How?"

"I don't know. Everyone was rather vague when I asked. Darcy said something about him slipping in the men's room at the Tea Room."

"Wow. That just leaves Henry to run everything."

Don't push too hard. "He could use you, Sam. Come home."

His sigh was audible. "I'm useless... to everybody."

Even though she knew he couldn't see it, Hannah shook her head. "That's not true. Don't talk that way. You're hurt, okay, but you're not useless." *At least not to me.*

"Really? Name one thing I could do."

Hold me? Share your life with me? "You're smart. You know how things work here on the farm. You could coach, direct, schedule..."

"In other words, be a paper pusher? No, thanks."

"They need you, Sam." *But not as much as I do.* "Why don't you move back?"

Hannah could hear his breath, slow and measured. "I don't think I'll ever be back."

Rhonda had warned her he wasn't planning on coming home, but hearing Sam verbalize it made her vision a little blurry. "I wish you'd reconsider."

She could swear she heard a sniffle. "I-I've got to get going."

"Why so soon? I've missed talking to you."

"My, uh, the TV, oh, I mean my cell's almost dead." He started making static noises. "Breaking up, can't you hear?"

"Right, *Scooter*."

The noises stopped. "Why'd you call me that?"

"Oh, someone told me you liked that name."

"Only two people ever called me that. And one of them's dead." His voice seemed tinged with anger.

Maybe I went too fast. "Sorry. Want to talk about it?"

"No. Gotta go now."

A heaviness began filling her chest. "Before you do, I need to say something."

Sam sighed again. "What?"

Hannah's nose and eyes were wet. "I miss you so much. Sam, I, I... " The words were on the tip of her tongue, but she wanted to say them in person. "Can I call you again, tomorrow?"

"Maybe not tomorrow. Riley's throwing a party tomorrow, you know, another of her weekly raves. Going to be loud and, uh, you know, kind of busy."

"I see. Missi really wants to say hi next time we talk. She misses her Samby."

Hannah wondered at the silence that ensued.

His voice was now quiet, almost a whisper. "Hannah? Do you think, I mean, is there any way, any chance we, you and I could..."

Her entire body tingled. "Yes?"

More silence followed. She knew he was struggling with something. "Forget it. Hey, thanks for calling, but I really need to go. Bye."

After he disconnected, Hannah leaned her head back against the pillow. At least this was a start. To help him. To let him see how much she needed him. To remind Sam that he needed her.

She closed her eyes, reminiscing about his smile. And her mind wandered, right up to the sixty-four thousand dollar question. *What was he going to ask before he hung up?*

Chapter 22

J ake slipped the bartender a five as thanks for the beer. The company Christmas party was well underway. Not where he wanted to be, but as a manager, he knew the CEO's expectations, that he needed to show his face. He strolled around the venue, looking for someplace inconspicuous to pass the time. All around him, his coworkers were laughing, telling stories and enjoying themselves. He found a secluded alcove to hide in. One where he could watch the festivities, but keep his distance.

The fragrance of the pine garland was a contrast to the scent of his brew. Jake closed his eyes, breathing deeply. *What are you doing tonight, Daisy?* His thoughts were interrupted by a woman's voice.

"Merry Christmas, Mr. Elliot. So you're hiding back here, all alone. Perhaps you're being a little anti-social tonight?" The woman was Amy Brighton, the Human Resources Manager. Her cheeks were flushed and when she came close, he could tell why. The alcohol on her breath was almost overwhelming.

"Evening, Ms. Brighton. No, I wasn't trying to avoid anyone." *Okay, that's a lie.* "I was just reminiscing about home and Christmases of yesteryear."

She studied him through her wire-rimmed, rectangular glasses. They gave her the appearance of being cross-eyed. *She's got to be drunk.* "Please, call me Amy. You miss Pennsylvania, Jake, don't you?"

"A little. Especially during the holiday season. My parents made this time of year special for me. We had our little traditions, ones I miss immensely."

Amy touched his hand. Hers was warm. "Are they still alive? Your parents, I mean."

Jake's throat choked up a little and he pulled back his hand. "No. Dad passed almost two years ago—cancer. Mom made it nine months longer. Pretty sure she died of a broken heart."

"I'm sorry, Jake. Is there a significant other in your life?"

He had to look away. "Not anymore. My ex-wife's getting married on New Year's Eve, in Paris. Some guy old enough to be her grandfather. And rich enough to own California." *Not to mention Daisy.* He drew a deep breath. "How about you? Where's home?"

Amy gazed at him for a while before answering. Maybe to decide if he was worthy of sharing. "Fredericksburg, Texas. Got married right out of college to my high school sweetheart. Lasted two years... which was about one year longer than we deserved. Colin was a hard-headed rancher and I was a knuckleheaded girl, bent on living life my way, not his. Didn't really have that much in common." She shook her head. "He remarried three days after our divorce was final." She took a long sip of her drink. "Did I mention he married my twin sister?"

"Wow. That had to hurt."

"You have no idea." She drained the rest of her glass. "Can I ask a pointed question?"

This ought to be good, since she's plastered. "Sure."

"You want to get out of here? I mean, we see these people every day. What do you say we blow this crackerjack stand? I live right down the road. We can have a lot more fun at my place."

His eyes opened wide. "Ms. Brighton..."

"Jake, please call me Amy."

"Okay, Amy. I'm not sure this is a great idea. We're both managers, so couldn't this be considered a conflict of interest?"

She shifted her weight. "Let me answer you clearly. A, we're not in a reporting relationship, so there's no conflict. B, I'm not asking for a commitment. C, I wasn't talking about sleeping together or a one-night stand. Furthest thing from my mind. I was thinking maybe we could watch a movie, or talk or play a game. Anything to get out of here. I'm tired of this crowd. What do you think?"

For the first time, he noticed Amy's irises were blue. *Daisy's blue eyes were clearer, prettier.* A pang of loneliness rippled through his chest. "My heart's not into being here, either. Maybe a cup of coffee and some conversation would be all right."

A smile slowly spread across her face. Amy opened her purse and retrieved a coat check coupon. "Mind getting my jacket while I powder my nose?"

"Okay." He watched her walk away. Amy was a very well built and attractive girl. Jake knew he should feel something for her, but the only thing he felt was the pain in his chest. Where Daisy Good had ripped his heart out. A hole that could never be filled again.

***

"Love you too, Mom. Give Dad my best. And yes, Riley and I will Facetime with you tomorrow." His lips sported a smile even though he was rolling his eyes. "Nope. Riley doesn't have a single Christmas cookie in the apartment." *Not anymore. I ate them all.* "Yes, I promise we're eating healthy. Mom, sorry. I've got to go to the bathroom. Love you, too. Merry Christmas. Bye."

Sam pocketed his cell. He hadn't lied, at least not about everything. His back teeth were floating. The crutches were cold as he hobbled to the bathroom. Sam pulled his cell from his pocket. *She* hadn't called yet, but it was still early.

Their daily talks had grown in length. He needed to hear her voice and she seemed to want to hear his. Sam needed her like he needed air to breathe. But Hannah's calls were bittersweet. She was right. Hannah was his best friend, ever. He missed seeing her, immensely. But he knew things would never turn out the way he wanted. No holding her tightly in his arms. No feel of her hand in his. No exploring those pretty lips while running his hands through that silky strawberry blonde hair. *Because I'm just a kid.*

The apartment shuddered. Sam worked his way to the window. He could barely make out the building across the street because of the swirling snow driven by the powerful wind. It was what the weather girl Miana referred to as a "lake effect" storm. A vision of Jenna's face filled his mind. He wouldn't be able to go on if something happened to Riley. *Please watch over my sister.* Why she had to go out today was beyond his imagination. The station seemed to take advantage of her every time they could. *A public event on Christmas Eve?* Riley probably pulled the duty slot because she was single. Always seemed his sister and her friend Didi got the short end of the stick.

As Sam watched a city bus trying to navigate through the mess, a vision came to him. Of Hannah. And a beautifully decorated tree. Their tree. Beth playing with her kitten and Missi on his lap. Hannah's smile was so beautiful. Her lips brushed his cheek as she set the tray down. One filled with hot chocolate and that special cake she made for him. The spice cake infused with coconut, triple chocolate icing and white drizzle. And who could forget the cherries? The emptiness in his heart welled up. *Love you. Need you so badly, Hannah. Gotta hear your voice.*

Hannah had moved back to her apartment the previous week. That was probably why she hadn't called yet. Sam's hands were shaky as he speed-dialed her. It only rang once before a female's voice came on. "Sam!"

Unfortunately, it wasn't the one he expected. "Oh, hi Beth. Merry Christmas. How ya doing?"

"Well hello, Sam. I haven't talked to you in way too long. Miss me?"

"Uh, sure."

"Cool. Guess what."

"I don't know. What?"

"It's snowing. We're having a white Christmas."

"Good. We are, too." Sam cleared his throat. "Can I talk to your mom?"

"She's indisposed at the moment. Said not to bother her."

That sounded strange. "What's she doing?"

"Who knows? She and John have been back in her bedroom for about an hour, locked door no less. Not sure what's happening in there, but there's an awful lot of whispering and laughing going on."

It was as if the world stopped. *She's hooked up with someone her own age. And I'm just a kid.* Sam could guess what was taking place in there. His life might as well be over. *Fine.*

"Sam, you still there?"

"Uh, yeah. Hey, I need to go. Been nice talking to you."

"You don't have to go yet. I'll keep you company."

Sam shook his head. "Sorry. I'm, uh, baking cookies and need to get them out of the oven."

"Should I tell Mom to call you back?"

And have Hannah know he knew what was going on in her bedroom with Selena's dad? "No. Merry Christmas."

"You, too. Wait. Missi wants to say hi."

Sam was going to lose it. "Can't right now. Talk to you later." He hung up and threw the device into the corner. "How could I have been so stupid? Believing she could care for *me*?"

A series of sharp raps on the apartment door interrupted his pity party. Sam hoisted himself up and tottered to the door. There were sobs coming from the hallway. He unlocked the door and swung it open. The beautiful blonde girl standing in the hallway had tears on her cheeks. Her words were choppy. "Can I come in? Please? I need a friend." It was Didi.

***

"There. Finally finished." John picked up his tools and dropped them in the satchel he'd brought.

Hannah struggled to push the newly assembled bike into the closet. "Thanks. It would have taken me forever. Missi will be so surprised. She asked Santa for a bike, you know?" Hannah turned to see John watching her.

"You're a great mom, Hannah. Your girls are lucky. So's that boy."

Hannah's chest tingled. "Boy?"

John scratched his chin as he watched her reaction. "Yeah. The one you love. What was his name? Sam?"

Her cheeks warmed. "Uh-huh."

John nodded. "Yep. Damned lucky kid. Well, I think I'll go. Taking Selena to my in-laws tonight for dinner. Wish all of you a very Merry Christmas."

"Thanks, John." She opened the bedroom door for him.

He called to his daughter, "Come on, kid. The way it's snowing, roads are gonna be slick. Let's give ourselves some extra time."

After the pair left, Hannah turned to her girls. "Anyone in the mood for spaghetti?"

Beth shrugged her shoulders. "Sounds good to me."

But when Hannah turned to Missi, she was greeted with crossed arms and a bottom lip that was sticking out, almost to the floor. "What's wrong, baby? You know Santa will be here in a few hours, so you better be good."

"I'm mad."

"Why are you mad, honey?"

"Samby wouldn't talk to me."

Hannah's mouth went dry. *Samby? Did he call?* "He wouldn't talk to you? When?"

Beth answered. "He called about a half hour ago. Didn't have much to say. He asked to speak with you, but I said you were busy. I told him Missi wanted to say 'hi', but all he wanted to do was hang up."

No, God, no. "Exactly what did you tell him I was busy doing?"

"I didn't know. I told him you and John were back in your bedroom."

Oh no. He probably misinterpreted that. "Where's my phone?"

Beth pointed across the room. "Over there, why?"

Hannah didn't bother answering. She quickly dialed Sam's number. "Pick up, Sam. Please pick up." But after four rings, it went to voicemail.

***

Sam used his crutch to push the apartment door open. "Come in, Didi. What's wrong?"

"I think I'm having a panic attack. It's... it's my first Christmas away from home. Had a bad dream last night that I never saw my family again. Then when I tried to call them, there was no answer. I'm scared, Sam."

I understand. "Have a seat, kiddo. It's probably nothing." It took a bit of convincing, but he finally talked her off the ledge. "This is my first yuletide away from home, too."

"But you have Riley. I don't have anyone. I can't stand the thought of being alone at Christmas."

Sam couldn't identify her perfume, but he liked it. His heart went out to her. So cute. Beautiful blue eyes. He offered his hand and she took it, very firmly. "Yes, you do. You have me... I mean, us. Spend it here. I'm sure Riley won't mind."

Didi's expression changed. *Hopefulness?* "You sure?"

Maybe he should have asked first, but his sister had a heart of gold and she spoke kindly of her friend. "Of course. So where's home?"

"Grand Rapids, South Dakota. My parents have a pizza shop there."

"So what number did you call?"

"Mom's cell. The shop always closes early on Christmas Eve."

"Maybe something changed. Try calling the restaurant. Possibly they're still there."

"Good idea." Didi walked into the bathroom to place her call.

As she did, Sam heard another phone ringing—his. The device was still in the corner where he'd tossed it. He ambled over, reaching it after the unit had stopped sounding. Hannah's name was on the display. *We have nothing to talk about, anymore. Hope you enjoyed your booty call.* He powered down the phone.

Didi's voice sounded happy as she re-entered the room. "I'm glad I got ahold of you. Merry Christmas and I'll call you tomorrow. I love you, Mom." Her face was full of happiness. To Sam's surprise, she gave him a quick hug. "Thanks for the suggestion. They had a big party come in just as they were about to close." She reached for his hand.

Sam touched Didi's fingers. So warm, so soft. He could see the relief on her face. "So everything's okay?"

"Yes. Thank you." Her expression faded and her lip quivered. "Were you serious earlier?"

He could get lost in those eyes. "About?"

"Me staying here, with both of you, tonight?"

Something warm started in his chest. *Riley said she had a crush on me.* "Absolutely." He shot a glance at the wall clock. "My sis told me she'd be home around ten. That gives us four hours. Want to do something?"

Didi's eyes grew wide. "It's going to sound crazy, but every year, my family watches the *Christmas Story*. Would you mind if we did that tonight?"

The thought of spending time with Didi was becoming more appealing by the second. *It'll take my mind off of Hannah.* "Sure."

"I'll pour us a soda or something if you find it on the television, okay?"

Sam could only smile and nod. Didi headed off to the kitchenette. *What do her lips taste like?* His heart was beating loudly as he watched her walk away. *This might be my best Christmas ever.*

Chapter 23

H annah was frantic. She could only imagine what was running through Sam's mind. *Turn your phone on, Sam.* His body might be hundreds of miles away, but he was here, right now, at the forefront of her mind. It took all her self-control to concentrate on making Christmas Eve somewhat normal for her girls. Hannah read a bedtime story about the nativity to Missi while Beth played with her cat. She finally finished the story.

"Okay, young lady. Time to get in bed and close your eyes. If you don't get to sleep, Sam won't come tonight."

Beth eyed her strangely. "Sam won't come tonight?"

Hannah's face heated. *Freudian slip.* "I meant Santa."

While Hannah tucked Missi in, Beth popped a *Jurassic Park* flick into the Blu-ray. Beth was infatuated with the whole scary dinosaur genre. Hannah slipped into the bathroom. Again, she dialed Sam's number. For the umpteenth time, it went straight to voicemail. *Now what?* She needed to talk to him, right this second—time was of the essence. A thought yelled out. *Call Riley.*

Sam probably didn't realize how often Hannah spoke to his sister. Riley was kind and caring, just like her mother. And she knew both Espenshade women were in her corner. With shaking hands, she called Sam's big sister.

"Hannah? Merry Christmas." There was piano music in the background.

"M-Merry Christmas to you, too. Hate to bother you, but are you with Sam?"

Laughter. "No. I'm covering a party for the station. Something wrong?"

Hannah's vision wasn't clear. "Riley, I screwed up." Hannah offloaded her fears.

Riley's voice wasn't as merry as before. "He probably has his phone turned off. He does that sometimes. I'll get back to the apartment around ten. I'll tell him to call you. Don't worry, Hannah. After you explain, I'm sure he'll understand."

"I can only guess what he thought was going on, but Riley, he's everything..." She couldn't complete the sentence.

Riley's voice was soft. "I know, Hannah. I'll help him understand. He needs you, and down inside, he knows it."

"I hope so."

"He does. And if he forgets, I'll remind him. I'll make sure he calls you tonight. Talk to you soon."

"Bye-bye." *God, help him understand.*

***

"Thanks for lending me these to sleep in." Didi was wearing a pair of his gym shorts and a comfy tee-shirt. The short, tight fitting floral print dress had looked uncomfortable and she jumped at his offer for something more casual to wear. Of course she'd had to cinch the shorts with a belt because of her slim build. *Doesn't matter what she wears, she's hot.*

The cable station was running the movie non-stop for a full day. Not Sam's favorite, but being this close to Didi held his interest. She was not only pretty, but she was funny. Talkative, but not overbearing. *And she smells good.*

"Want another pillow for your leg?"

And so kind to boot. "I'm good."

"Again, thanks for letting me stay with you two. And for watching this movie. Corny, I know, but it's a family tradition." She turned to study his face. "Tell me about growing up back east."

A cloud blotted out the happiness. "I had a great childhood. My parents were wonderful. And my sisters..." *Sisters. Only Riley's left.*

Didi took his hand. "Riley told me about Jenna, how close you were. I'm so sorry."

Sam bit his lip. "Thanks, I'd rather not..."

"I understand. Didn't mean to pry. Want to watch something else?"

"Up to you."

A sly expression slowly covered her face. "Of course, we could *do* something else..."

Is she flirting? A warmth filled Sam's chest. "Like what?"

"Twenty questions?" Her countenance changed. "If the answer's no, I get it. And I didn't mean dirty things. I just want to find out more about you, and have you get to know me, that's all."

His mind drifted back to Hannah. She had closely guarded her past. And here he had someone who actually wanted to share information about her life with him. "Okay. I'm game." He turned off the television.

When her lips curled into a smile, the brilliance of her white teeth showed through. "Sam, I appreciate your spontaneity. Can I go first?"

Sam found himself fighting back the urge to laugh. "Be my guest."

"Favorite color?"

"Red. Yours?"

"Hot pink. Number?"

"Seven."

Didi wrinkled her nose as she studied him. "Mine is nine. You ask."

Without a thought, the question rolled off his tongue. "First kiss?"

"Senior prom. Gary Quinn."

"Was it good?"

"Sam!"

"I'm sorry."

She squeezed his hand and looked away. "Not really. Believe it or not, that was the only time anyone kissed me. I'm really shy. And not very bright. I had to study really hard just to graduate."

Sam's eyes grew large. "I wouldn't ever have thought that, you know, you had trouble. I love how you come across on the tube. Thought you were a brainiac."

Didi's smile grew. "You, you watch me on the news?"

His face heated. "Y-yes. I watch you... and Riley, of course."

She drew a deep breath. "Why?"

Because you're cute. "I... I don't know."

Her lips turned into a smirk. "Samuel Espenshade! Are you lying to me?"

Why do women always insist on calling me Samuel? "Uh, maybe..."

"I thought so. We'll come back to this later. Your turn. First kiss?"

She just let me off the hook. "Ashley Snyder, Valentine's Day a couple of years ago."

She winked at him. *Flirtatiously?* "On a date? And was it only one kiss?"

"Not a date. I was just spending time with her. She had cancer and it wasn't looking good. The chemo took her hair, so I shaved my head, for support. Told me she doubted she'd live long enough to kiss anyone. And yes, only one kiss."

Didi frowned and her eyes seemed watery. "That was kind. Did she live?"

"Yes. Ash is doing very well."

Her smile returned. "Great. Your turn to ask a question."

"You smell so good. What's that scent?"

Didi's eyes seemed to shine. "You like it?" Sam nodded. "Plumeria. My parents took me to Hawaii when I was a teenager and I fell in love with it. The flowers are beautiful, too."

Just like you. They continued to talk, but Sam could tell she was tiring. "Early mornings catching up to you?"

She nodded. "Sorry. It's not because you're boring, or," she yawned, "that I don't like you." She touched the side of his face with her fingers. "I think you're very special." Didi's light touch drew his lips toward hers. His eyes closed as her essence filled his very soul. Sam leaned forward in anticipation of their first kiss.

The slam of the apartment door broke the spell. Riley's hands were on her hips and the anger was apparent to both of them. Her face was red, except for the white line of her lips. "Would one of you like to explain to me what's going on here?"

***

The roads had been rough, but passable. Riley was relieved when she parked her Escape in the lot next to a car that was the same model as Didi Phillips'. She momentarily pondered the possibility Didi was visiting with Sam. *No, she wouldn't.* Even though her friend had a massive crush on him, Riley had made it clear someone special was waiting for him back east. She'd told Didi that Sam was off-limits.

Riley's jaw almost hit the floor when she entered the apartment. She noted Didi's fingertips on Sam's cheek and how her brother was responding. *No!* She slammed the door and barked out her question. Both of them had deer in the headlight looks on their faces. "I'm waiting for a response."

Sam's face was blood red. "I, uh, I mean, uh, Didi stopped by. She was like, all alone tonight. Her first Christmas by herself, so, I invited her to spend the night. With us."

You mean with you. Riley's vision was red-tinged. "Oh, and you did this without consulting me?"

Didi's face was red, too. "I'm sorry. I'll just, uh, leave." She turned to Sam. "Thanks for your hospitality, Sam."

Riley forced herself to calm down. "No, you can stay. I was just shocked to come home and find you not only wearing my brother's clothes, but to discover you two making out. I don't even do that here and it's my apartment!" The younger girl was wiping her cheeks. *She's your friend.* Riley drew a deep breath. "If my brother invited you to stay, then don't leave. But you'll sleep in *my* room, not out here."

"Sorry, Riley. I believe it would be better if I left."

I'm more upset with Sam than you. Riley walked over and hugged her friend. "No. Stay. My bed's more comfortable anyway. I'll sleep out here with my brother."

Didi's eyes were questioning her. "You sure?"

"Absolutely. Just let me change out of my dress and grab a few things."

Riley made it quick and waited until the other girl closed the bedroom door before she turned to Sam and addressed him harshly. "What were you thinking?"

He used those puppy dog eyes he usually reserved for Mom and Dad when he was getting chewed out. "I was just trying to be nice to *your* friend. She was sad."

"I'm not talking about that. If I didn't walk in when I did, you were going to kiss her, and I can only guess what was going to happen next." He acted shocked. "Don't act stupid with me. Did you forget about Hannah?"

His face paled. "I'm nothing to her. I tried to call her tonight and you know what she was doing? She and that stupid neighbor of hers were getting it on, with her daughters in the next room."

Riley shook her head. "Really? Is that what Beth told you?"

"Y-yes. Just in not so many words."

"Liar. She told you they were in the bedroom, laughing and whispering, not that they were fooling around."

Sam's eyes grew wide. "How do you know that?"

"Because when you acted childish and turned off your phone, Hannah called me."

His lips turned white as he drew them into a thin line. "I thought so."

"Thought what?"

"You talk to her a lot, don't you? And *you* were the one who told her my nickname was Scooter."

It's out of the bag now. "As a matter of fact, Hannah and I have talked quite a bit lately, because my only brother is *dumb.*"

Sam started to raise his voice. "You and Mom can't help but stick your noses in my business. You have no right to..."

She shushed him. "Keep your voice down. This is between you and me and I don't want Didi to hear us. And yes, I do have a right to look out for you, because you're too immature to act like a man. Come on, Sam. Are you an idiot? Hannah's in love with you."

"Right. She loves me so much she just couldn't contain herself. Next you'll tell me he was only a surrogate for me because I wasn't there."

Riley had to breathe deeply to calm herself. "Such a big man, aren't you? A know-it-all. You think you're so smart, but you don't know anything. Call her and ask her exactly what happened."

"I'm never talking to that slut again."

Riley slapped her brother so hard her fingers hurt. "Don't you *ever* call Hannah that again."

Sam's cheek was pink and he rubbed it. "You girls always stick together, don't you?"

"Only the ones who care about you. God alone knows why she does." She retrieved his phone and handed it to him. "Call Hannah, now."

"Give me one reason why I should."

Her eyes were suddenly scratchy. "Because you'd been stuck in a downward spiral since Jenna died. Hannah is what brought my brother back, gave him a reason to live. You two were meant for each other. Sam, everyone can see it. Can't you?"

Sam held his hands in front of him. "Don't bring Jenna into this. I'm never calling Hannah, ever."

What came next hurt her more than it possibly could him. "If you don't, you're leaving in the morning."

Sam's mouth dropped open. "Kicking me out? On Christmas morning? You wouldn't do that to me, would you? I thought you loved me."

"I love the man my brother *used* to be."

"But Riley, I don't have anywhere else to go."

She stuck the phone in his face. "Then I guess you better start dialing."

Chapter 24

J ake swirled the coffee around in his mug. *I should leave soon.*

"You're awfully quiet tonight."

The scent of pine and cinnamon awoke fond memories. Looking into Amy's blue eyes brought back the recollection of a time when he gazed into the most beautiful eyes he'd ever seen. *Where are you tonight, Daisy?*

Amy sipped her java and laughed. "I rest my case."

"Sorry. You haven't exactly been a chatterbox, either."

"Hmm. Guess you're right. I was sifting through my memories."

"Thinking about your ex-husband?"

Amy blew her nose. "Once upon a time, on a Christmas Eve long ago, Colin proposed to me." She wiped her cheek and forced back a sob. "Under the mistletoe."

"I'm sorry."

"Me, too, but enough about my problems. What about you? Thinking about your ex?"

"Not really. I'm over her."

"Your parents?"

"Maybe a little."

Amy touched his hand. "That's not what's bothering you, is it?"

Jake glanced out the window. The snow was heavier than the last time he'd looked.

"You can talk to me. I owe you for the other night."

"No, Amy, you don't."

"Lesser men would have taken advantage of me, seeing how drunk I was."

"Wasn't raised that way. Always be respectful and kind. Give the benefit of the doubt." *Like you did with Daisy?* He shook away the thought.

"Well, thanks anyway. I was having a really hard time. I'd just found out my twin sister's expecting. That should have been Colin and me, not her. All because I was so, so damned righteous. Had it in my mind I was right and he was wrong. Never gave him a chance to explain himself." She wiped her eyes. "I let the love of my life go, because I was stubborn."

The coffee suddenly wasn't sitting so well in his stomach. *Sounds familiar, doesn't it?* "Yes."

Amy sniffed. "Yes to what?"

"I'm sorry. Answering the voices in my head."

Amy laughed through her tears. "I thought I was the only one they spoke to. Tell me about her."

Jake swallowed hard. Her face flashed before him and he paused before responding to Amy. "Daisy. Her name is Daisy, and she's perfect. She loved me, once upon a time." Now his eyes were blurry.

Amy rubbed his arm. "Is it too late?"

He sighed and looked away. "Pretty sure it is. Hey, I gotta go. It's really getting deep outside." Jake stood.

Amy wiped her nose with a tissue. "Some pair we are, huh?"

"Guess so."

"Text me when you get home, and thanks. It would have been a lonely night with just my memories to keep me company."

Jake nodded. "Appreciated you being here, too."

She touched his cheek, speaking quietly. "A word of advice, my friend. If it's not too late, go to her and patch it up. Don't be stuck with a life of regret, like I am. I'd give anything to have a chance to do it over again." She reached up and kissed his cheek. "'Night, Jake. Merry Christmas."

"You, too."

The wind cut through his jacket, chilling his bones. But the icy feelings running rampant up and down his spine weren't caused by the wind. Instead, it was the words Amy had whispered. *Is it really too late?* He climbed into his truck. With trembling hands, he pulled out his cell. Five minutes to midnight. *Should I call?* Without waiting for an answer, he dialed her number from memory. *Pick up, Daisy. I need to hear your voice.* He couldn't wait to talk to her.

But it wasn't Daisy that answered. Instead, it was a message. "The number you have dialed is no longer in service."

Jake stared at the device. "What? Must've dialed the wrong number." He pulled up Daisy's contact and pressed her number. When the same message came on, Jake dropped the phone. "It can't be too late. There's got to be a way to find her."

***

The twinkling lights on the tree were beautiful, but Hannah didn't see them. In her mind's eye, Sam's smile taunted her. *My life sucks.* It started when her mother abandoned her and continued when she drank that beer at Dale Olphin's stupid party. Hannah shivered as she tried to force the memories out of her mind. But one prevailed— waking up in a cornfield, pregnant. No idea who the father was. Losing her husband. And now this, this *thing* between her and Sam.

She sipped her eggnog. It was lukewarm. Her aunt had wanted her to have an abortion and told her she'd kick Hannah out the day the child was born if she refused. "Thank you, God, for not letting me do that." If she had, Beth wouldn't be here today.

Reach out to me, Sam. We need to talk. The clinking of chains and flashing yellow lights flowed through the window. The Township was out treating the roads. It was now officially Christmas morning. Riley should have talked to Sam a couple of hours ago. Riley told her Cleveland was getting pelted by heavy snow. Hopefully his sister was all right. *Please keep Riley safe.*

Hannah placed her cell phone on the coffee table and headed to the bathroom. *Please call me, Sam.* She had to speak with him, to explain what had happened. She needed to hear his voice or she'd go crazy.

The whistle from her phone indicated a text message. Hannah rushed to retrieve her device. There was a text from Sam!

U still up? Riley told me to call you.

She quickly texted back.

Yes! ☺ Can I call?

Her phone rang almost immediately. "Hannah?"

Her palms were sweaty. "Sam. So glad to hear your voice. Merry Christmas."

"Yeah. Same to you. Riley made me call. So what do you want?" His voice was tinged with annoyance, something she'd expected.

"I know you called earlier. And Beth told me what she said."

"So? You're a big girl."

"I need to explain what was going on."

He snorted. "I'm pretty sure I know. You enjoy your booty call?"

I need to make you understand. "It wasn't like that. Nothing happened."

"Like I care. You don't have to fill me in on all the juicy details."

"Sam, I want to explain. I need to."

"Laughter and whispers behind locked doors. For over an hour? Such a lucky girl."

No! "John was only helping me assemble Missi's Christmas present—her bike."

"Sure. Whatever."

She drew a deep breath. "I'm telling you the truth."

"Uh-huh."

"Stop it right now and listen. You've grown to know me over the last couple of months, better than anyone ever has. Think of how close we've become. I hope you trust me. Do you really think I'd do that to you?"

"Oh no. You'd never do *that* with me. I'm just a kid in your mind. And besides, I don't really know you. Every time I've asked about your past, you kept it from me."

It was becoming difficult to focus on the tree. The lights were blurry. "One thing at a time. I know you overheard my conversation with Kyle. And yes, I did say you were just a kid."

His voice came through loud and clear. "I know. Heard you say it. Just statin' how you felt, right?"

"No. What's happening between you and me was none of Kyle's business. Look, I don't want to argue. I guarantee, if it was just you and me talking, I wouldn't have answered that way."

Ice was wrapped around his words. "That's easy to say, *now*."

"Try me. Ask me how I feel about you. Right this second and I'll pour out my heart."

Silence. "I don't think that's a good idea."

"Why?"

"Because."

His immaturity was so frustrating. "Why? Because of what you're afraid I'll say or because it might change your mind and you won't be pissed anymore? I know you're upset. You think I cheated on you."

"You don't have to explain. And cheated on *me*? I have *no* claim on you."

The fingers of her free hand were white as she clamped them together. "Yes, you do. You're my best friend."

"Right. Quit saying things you don't mean, Hannah."

"Why are you being so obstinate? If the roles were reversed, I'd listen to you."

"You mean, like to hear my side of things?"

Was there a light at the end of the tunnel? "Exactly. To find out what really happened and hear your side of the story."

"I see. You mean like you did when you thought I was stealing from the company, and ratted on me to Henry and Harry?"

Her jaw clenched. *He just wants to argue.* "We talked about that. You were the one who wouldn't talk to me then."

More silence. "You made your point." He sighed hard enough that she could almost feel the breeze. "Go ahead and tell me what happened so it'll make *you* feel better."

"Thank you. I bought a bike for Missi, but it required assembly. That's why I asked John to come over. He put it together for her. That's why we were in my bedroom."

"Um-hmm. How'd you pay him back? With your kisses, or maybe more, huh? Is that why all the whispering?"

It was her turn to be silent. "Obviously you don't believe or trust me."

"Why should I? You're a beautiful woman. He's a lonely man. And the holidays make it the perfect recipe for a... a... you know what. Uh, forget it. Do you mean to tell me the thought of sleeping with him didn't even cross your mind? Or his?"

Hannah swallowed, hard. "He did make a pass, but I made it clear, right away, it wasn't happening. My heart belongs to someone else."

"So you want me to believe you spent over an hour locked in your bedroom with him and the two of you didn't even kiss or touch or fool around?"

Disappointment flowed down her arms. "You think that little of me?"

"Give me a reason not to."

Hannah's voice was gentle. "Sam, think of how much time we've spent together. You know me, inside and out, better than anyone *ever* has. Am I really that kind of girl?"

His breathing was coming quickly. She knew he was fumbling for words. "Like I said, I don't know you. You never really let me in."

"You should talk. I understand there's a lot *you* haven't told me. About your accident, for example."

He growled through the air waves. "Some things are private."

"So, is that the way you want to play this? I could say the same thing right back to you, too. Want honesty? Here you go. Ask me now, anything you want and I'll tell you everything you could possibly want to know."

"Anything?"

"I didn't stutter. Try me."

He grew quiet. "Tell me about your marriage."

Her response was immediate. "Dave was a very kind man. We married when I was seventeen. He was forty-two." She expected Sam would be floored by what she just said. *I need to explain.* But before she could say anything, Sam exploded.

"What? Forty-two minus seventeen is twenty-five. I don't understand. You married someone way, way older than you? Why?"

Hannah drew a deep breath. She noted a cobweb in the corner of the room. Hannah shuddered, expecting another explosive reaction. "Sam, I was pregnant. It wasn't Dave's child, and his proposal was my only option. There was no other choice. It was hard, but we made it work."

Disbelief. "Wait. Not his kid? Then whose was it?"

You don't know how much it hurts to tell you. She'd never told anyone, except Dave, the truth. Beth didn't even know. "I, I'm not sure."

"What? You don't know? What the heck does that mean? Were you some party girl? How many guys did you get it on with?"

Hannah was having trouble holding back the sobs. "I went to a party. Someone must have slipped something in my beer. My next clear memory was two weeks later. I woke up in a cornfield, and later found out I was pregnant. I have very few recollections of what happened during that time, only blurry nightmarish visions of being beaten and repeatedly abused." She wiped her eyes. "What else do you want to know, Sam? Keep asking and I'll answer, anything to satisfy your curiosity."

His voice softened. "I'm sorry. Let's stop this, now. This should be a face to face conversation, not one for the phone."

Hannah sniffed. "I agree. When do you plan on coming home?"

Sam sighed. "I don't plan on coming back to Lancaster, ever."

"Then tell me where you'll be, where you're moving to."

"Why?"

"Because wherever you go, I'll be there."

"Again, why?"

"Do I need to spell it out to you, what you mean to me, and my girls? I've never felt as alive as I do when I'm with you. Do you need me to tell you in plainer words? Samuel Espenshade, I'm in—"

His next words were quick, but sad. "Don't. Not now. Sorry I pushed you. Should never have asked." Sam sniffled. "Wish I could undo this conversation." Momentary silence. "Oh, look at how late it is. I'll leave you go, so you can sleep."

"Like I'll be able to. Don't go, Sam. It's Christmas. Please don't hang up like this. Let's talk this out, the whole thing."

"Hannah, I've got to go."

"Not yet, please? I'm begging you."

"No. I need to think, to understand this. It's too... Goodbye. Merry Christmas."

I'll go crazy if it ends like this. Hannah's arms were trembling. "You asked for the truth and I gave it to you. Do you know how hard that was?"

"I don't mean to—"

"You once told me you wanted to earn my total trust. Do you think I would have told you about what happened if I you didn't have my total trust?"

Sam was quiet, but Hannah could hear his breathing, deep and unsteady. After a long pause, he continued. "Hannah, I gotta go, please?"

Frustration filled her body. "You're a man, Sam. You've proved that. Now it's time to act like one!"

His voice was breaking. "I can't right now. Just... "

"Just what?"

She heard sniffing on the other end of the line. "I'm sorry, Hannah. I'm hanging up now."

"No. You love me, Samuel Espenshade. I feel it. Your mother and sister see it. But for whatever reason, you ran off to Cleveland, like a little boy. I wish you'd open your eyes and heart and talk to me. Or did you forget we're best friends?"

Sam's words were measured. "You do not understand. I can *not* talk about this right now. I need time, to process my feelings. I'm saying goodbye right now."

She'd lost the battle. "Fine! Will you at least call me tomorrow, so we can talk more, please? I can't take this distance between us anymore. It's time to get past it or forget everything." He was silent. "Are you going to call me tomorrow?"

A long hesitation. "We'll see. 'Night." With those words, the phone went silent. Hannah's fell to the floor.

Chapter 25

S am found sleep almost impossible to come by. *I'm an idiot.* Poor Hannah, suffering through something so horrible. *And what did I do?* Treated her like pond scum, like she was nothing. Forced her to relive her nightmare. *I know how it feels to go through misery, again.*

For the longest time, he simply listened to the howl of the wind outside. *She deserves someone much better than me.* He was unworthy of her friendship, her trust, and her love.

The last look at the clock read three in the morning. Sleeping on an afghan a few feet away was Riley. His sister's rhythmic breathing finally lulled him to sleep.

All at once, he was back on the diamond. The smell of fresh cut grass and buttered popcorn filled his senses. It was the last game of the playoffs. And the big league coach was there, to see Sam's performance. And so far, Sam had done very well, if he had to say so himself. Four hits in four at bats, a double, a triple and two home runs. He'd thrown out three base runners on steals and picked off one runner at first. Sam had driven in all nine runs on the scoreboard. He was facing a full count and the bases were loaded. Down by three runs with two outs in the last inning and the great Sammy Espenshade—the winning run—was at the plate. The moment he'd dreamed of all his life was before him. After tightening up his batting glove, he dug his left toes into the dirt in the batter's box and then planted his right foot. Bat over his shoulder, he was ready for the delivery.

From the stands, Jenna's voice was louder than everyone else as she rooted for him. A smile covered his face. The pitcher shook off the first two calls by the catcher, then nodded. This was it, his appointment with destiny and he knew what to expect, what he would call. *Fastball.*

The opposing pitcher wound up and delivered a rocket, just on the outside of the plate, knee high. Sam swung, the jolt of the ball against his bat sending shock waves up his arms. The horsehide began its ascent toward outer space. Sam couldn't move. Standing in the batter's box, he was mesmerized. In the distance, the left fielder started to turn, then hung his head. Sam's eyes followed the ball, holding his breath until the white object disappeared beyond the stadium wall. Sam kissed the bat, threw it to the batboy and began his trot around the bases.

The cacophony of noise was deafening as he rounded first. Cheers filled the air. "Sammy, Sammy, Sammy." By the time he turned second, the other team was leaving the dugout for the locker room. Fans were competing with each other to stand in line along the third base stripe after he stepped on the base, hands outstretched to touch him.

Thirty feet from home plate, he stopped and dug his hands in his pocket. The crowd went wild as he did the 'Sammy Shuffle', his trademark homerun dance along the path to home plate. Finally, he stopped before jumping with both feet on the plate. The crowd erupted with so much noise his ears hurt.

His teammates lifted him to their shoulders, screaming, laughing, yelling and cheering. They deposited him right in front of the big league manager. The man extended his hand. "Well done, Espenshade. You just punched your ticket to spring training camp with the team. Report to pitcher and catcher camp in Florida on March second. See you there, and," the manager grinned and patted him on the back, "welcome to the show."

As soon as the man turned away, Sam's parents sandwiched him in their arms. "So proud of you, son."

Riley, his sister the sportscaster, was next, on the job as always. His sister shoved a microphone in his face. "So how does it feel to win it all and have your dreams come true, brother?"

His joy knew no end. "Favorite day of my life, ever."

Before he could say more, Jenna slammed into him and engulfed Sam in a hug. "We did it, Scooter. Never been prouder of you than right now."

He held Jenna tightly. "It's all because of you. Thanks. Best moment of my life."

Her smile was beautiful. "Not yet. It's about to get better." Her eyes searched his. Her voice was barely a whisper. "She's waiting on you, at home plate."

He was confused. Even though Sam was aware this was only a dream, he knew this part hadn't happened that way. "Someone's waiting on me?"

Jenna's smile was ear to ear. "Yes. Your true love is waiting and God allowed me to come back, so I could see it happen."

Sam turned toward the plate as everyone else disappeared. Standing in the batter's box was a woman in a lacy wedding dress, but a veil covered her face. She was holding a bouquet of flowers.

He walked to the woman. He couldn't see her features, but knew her voice immediately. "I've been here, all along. Waiting on you, Sam. Are you going to kiss me?"

His hands trembled as he lifted the veil. "Hannah?" She nodded and threw her arms around him.

"I've waited forever to do this. I love you, Samuel Espenshade." Her lips were sweet, warm and wet as the two of them melted together.

Sam pulled back enough to see her eyes. A woman's voice filled his ears, but it belonged to Jenna, not Hannah. "This is your destiny. Go to her, *right now, Scooter.*"

Hands were on his shoulder, shaking him. "Go to her? Who do you want to go to? Riley?" The voice was familiar but he couldn't make it fit.

Sam swallowed hard as he forced his eyes open. His breath was coming in rapid bursts. Though dressed in his clothes, the beautiful, golden haired female before him looked like she'd just stepped out of a glamour magazine photo shoot.

"Sam, wake up. Are you okay? You're talking in your sleep."

"Didi? What's happening? Where'd she go? She was right here, just a second ago."

Didi touched his nose. "Riley's in the kitchen, making breakfast. Can I get you anything?"

The taste of Hannah's lips lingered on his. "I don't mean Riley." Everything was suddenly clear. "Didi, help me. Can you get my laptop? It's on the end table over there."

"Uh, sure. Is that all?"

"No. My wallet's in the pocket of my jeans." He pointed to his suitcase in the corner. "Open up my luggage. They're right on top."

Sam whipped the top open on his computer and pounded on the keyboard.

Didi sat next to him, his wallet in her hand. "What are you doing?"

"Listening to my sister."

***

Hannah popped a pod into the Keurig. It was Christmas Night. She'd been unable to sleep after the call from Sam. Anticipating the conversation, she hadn't allowed her cell to leave her pocket. But when he hadn't called by lunch, she tried reaching him. Nothing. Her calls went right to voicemail. All of the texts she sent throughout the day went unanswered.

The coffee maker hissed as it finished depositing the bitter liquid in her cup. Hannah grabbed the container of Italian Sweet Cream from the fridge and poured until the liquid in her mug was the color of chalk. Her girls were both in bed. Despite her exhaustion, sleep wasn't going to come tonight. *Got to do something, or I'll lose my mind.* She opened her cupboards, collected the ingredients and started to mix a cake. It wasn't until she slid the pans into the oven that she realized what she'd done. She was baking Sam's favorite cake.

The lump in her throat didn't seem to go away, no matter how hard she swallowed. *He's through with me.* Sam had asked for the truth, and she gave it. But he was distancing himself. *He couldn't handle it.* Her chest ached. *How could you? Don't you know how much I need you? And love you?* But there was no answer.

The timer rang. Hannah opened the oven door, sticking a toothpick into the cakes. *They're done. Wish you were here to eat it with me, Sam.* It would never be. She knew in her heart of hearts she'd seen the last of him. After the cakes were cool enough, she injected the coconut liquid. Concentrating on whipping the triple chocolate icing to perfection took her mind off her troubles.

A knock sounded from the front door. Hannah glanced at the clock—quarter to eleven. Who in the world would come over at this time of night? Her heart quickly beat out of control. *Sam? Let it be Sam.* Hannah whipped open the door and her mouth fell to the ground when she recognized the man standing in the freezing night air. It was Sheriff Jed Olphin, Dale's brother.

Chapter 26

J ed Olphin dreaded this visit. He was cleaning up his brother's loose ends. The door swung open and the face he vaguely remembered turned pale. *I know why.* He tipped his hat. "Sorry to bother you so late, Hannah. Tried to get here yesterday, but with all the delays..." She was backing away, fear obvious in her expression.

"Wh-what do you want, with me?" Hannah's limbs were trembling.

"You're scared, but don't be. My brother lied to you. I'm not here to hurt you."

She was breathing rapidly as she stared at him. "But you hunted me down and found me anyway. I tried so hard not to leave a trail."

Jed still stood outside, in the cold night air. "You did good, Hannah. I've been looking for you for four months. Finally got a location when you opened that phone account."

Tears stained her cheeks as her expression turned into a frown. "Okay, you found me. Now what are you going to do? Please, please don't hurt my girls."

"I'm not going to hurt anyone. I came to pass on some information and hand over something that's rightfully yours."

"I don't understand. What information?"

Jed sighed. Sorrow filled his heart, but he couldn't decide if it was for Hannah or his brother. "My brother Dale passed away five months ago. Complications after routine surgery. Last couple weeks of his life were unbelievably miserable for him."

There was a change in the woman's expression. "You travelled all this way to tell me that your brother is dead? Should I really care?"

Jed studied the porch floor. "No. Just 'fore he died, Dale got religion." His eyes gravitated to engage hers. "Confessed all his sins. Told me how he drugged you at that party years ago and what he and his friends did. Also told me the lie he whispered to you about me. Hannah, I swear to God, I never touched you years ago and I never would have done any of the things he threatened you with. I'm sorry about that. That's why you ran, isn't it?"

The scent of something wonderful wafted out of the kitchen. The faint fragrance of coconut teased his nose. His mind drifted back to Hannah. Her chin was quivering. "It was bad enough, his come-ons to me, but when he threatened my daughters, I couldn't take the chance."

"Wish you would have told me. I'd have thrown him in jail, brother or not."

"Dale told me you were one of the men who abused me, years ago, and that you wanted to do it again."

Sadness filled his chest. "That was an out and out lie. I didn't and never would treat you or anyone else like that. But what happened to you did affect me. When they said you were missing, I volunteered. Helped search for you, praying I'd be the one who found you. After you were finally found, and then they couldn't solve your case, that's what made me want to become a lawman. To keep what happened to you from ever occurring again."

Hannah was shaking her head. "Please don't make me re-live that again."

Jed hung his head. "Sorry, didn't mean to. Bear with me just one more minute and I'll leave you alone for good." He unbuttoned his coat and retrieved an envelope from his shirt pocket. Jed handed it to her.

Hannah wiped her eyes and took the envelope. "What's this?"

"I told you Dale repented. Asked me to tell you he was sorry. Said he could never give back what he took from you. Prayed his last act on earth might make your life a little easier."

Hannah searched his eyes. "I don't know what you're talking about."

"Dale made you the sole beneficiary on his life insurance. The check's made out to you."

She shook her head and took the offered envelope. "No, I couldn't possibly. I mean..."

Jed took a step inside and touched her arm. "I'd give anything to erase what happened to you, but I can't. My brother was despicable and cruel, especially to you. This is his last chance to do a little good in this world. Use the money for your benefit, or for your girls." He could see the questions in her mind. Ones she'd have to work out. *Time to go.* "Goodbye, Hannah."

Jed backed out, tipped his hat and just before he closed the door, shot one last look at her. Hannah was staring at the envelope.

***

Hannah's hands shook so badly, she was afraid she'd drop the envelope. She sat on a chair and eased her fingernail under the lip. Sliding her nail along the slot, she liberated the piece of paper inside. Hannah's eyes grew wide when she read the amount of the check. *All those zeros? Must be some mistake.* Was this all for her? Maybe she could still catch Jed.

Hannah ran to the door and yanked it open. She had to take a step back. There *was* a man standing there, but it wasn't Jed. It was Sam Espenshade, supporting himself on a pair of crutches. The room started spinning just before it went black.

Someone was shaking her gently and calling her name. A man's voice. After the wild dream she'd had, she knew it couldn't be true.

"Hannah? Wake up, please? I can't carry you inside right now."

A freezing cold wind whistled up her pajama bottoms, chilling her thighs. And something was across her legs. Something firm and cold.

"Hannah, it's me. Open your eyes."

She had to concentrate really hard to force one eye open. Sitting on his behind was Sam Espenshade. *Sam? On my doorstep?* Her eyes reached further past his crutches, which were laid across her legs, until she could see snow swirling around the street lamp. She turned to view Sam's face. His eyes were intense and his face sported that crooked smile she thought she'd never see again. *What just happened?* Hannah uttered the first thought that entered her mind. "We don't live in a barn. Can't you at least close the door when you come in?"

Sam wrapped his arms around her and drew her close. "I'm sorry about yesterday... and how I've treated you since I got hurt. Can I explain why I acted like that to you?"

Hannah nodded. "Yes, yes. But can we close the door first?"

"I'll need help."

His broken leg! She'd forgotten. Hannah shook off the residual dizziness and not only closed the door, but helped Sam get seated on the couch. Her hands couldn't help touching his face. *Is this a dream?*

He was almost gasping for breath when he grabbed her hands. "I feel so bad about last night, forcing you to relive your past. For making you tell me what happened. What you went through."

"It's okay. I'll gladly tell you everything. I don't want anything between us, ever."

"I know. My turn now. This may not come out right, but I need you to hear it. Will you listen?"

Hannah nodded. His eyes were moist. *He's finally going to tell me about the accident.* "Only if you want to."

He held her face in his hands. "Friends like us share everything." He kissed her forehead, softly, before releasing her.

The world was spinning again, but in a good way. *Kiss me again!* His eyes encountered hers with a seriousness she'd never seen. Hannah realized she was looking at his heart and soul.

"Since I could walk, my life was baseball. Both my sisters used to play it with me, but Jenna made it her life's mission to help me be the best I could be. Countless hours of throwing a ball, batting and explaining the strategies. And somehow, I became good. Really, really good."

Sam squeezed her hands tightly. "Jenna saved up her money and bought me a pitching machine so I could practice catching and batting. She worked with me for hours every night. And it paid off. By the time I was fourteen, professional scouts were coming to my games. In my freshman year of high school, I made second string amateur All-American."

He paused. Hannah shook her head. "It sounds like she really loved you... and believed in you."

Sam's face screwed up. "She wasn't just my sister, she was my best friend. I miss her so much."

Hannah touched his face. "You don't have to do this if you don't want to."

Sam wiped his eyes and violently shook his head. "You deserve to know it all. While my family supported me, Jenna pushed me higher and harder, every day. So much so that I was the number one draft choice three years ago. My face was on the cover of *Sports Illustrated*. 'Sammy Espenshade—Baseball's Real Mr. Natural'."

"What? *Sports Illustrated?*"

His eyes were boring into her soul. He appeared not to have heard her. "Day after I graduated high school, I was playing double-A ball in the midwest.

Two weeks later, I moved up to triple-A. The sky was the limit. I could do no wrong. Led the league in every offensive and defensive statistic. My team even made it to the championship, because of me."

His hands were shaking so badly. She realized how hard this was. She'd gone through it last night. "It's all right," she said. "You don't have to..."

"Yes, I do. I made you tell me about your worst moment. My turn now. Long story short, I hit the walk-off homerun to win the pennant. And I did it in front of my family. In front of the one person who sacrificed the hardest to get me there—my sis, Jenna. The two of us took a couple of days to blow off some steam. Knew it might be one of the last times before everything changed. She was getting married in the spring and I was headed for the big leagues. We were both about to achieve our dreams, so Jenna and I celebrated and had the time of our lives. Then we headed home."

Oh my God. This is just before the accident. "Sam, honey, I know what happened. Your mom told me. Why don't we—"

Sam was staring at the floor. "We were less than two hours away, on the turnpike. Music blasting, we were singing our hearts out to Jason Aldean, when a deer ran in front of the car. Jenna swerved and the next thing I knew, we were tumbling down a mountain, hood over trunk and rolling side to side. When we slammed into a crevasse at the bottom, I passed out from the pain. My leg was broken and I was pinned in the car."

He stopped. Hannah wiped the moisture from his cheeks. "Honey, you don't..."

"The way the car was situated, Jenna was directly above me. I was covered in blood. Took me a while to realize it wasn't mine. It was hers. Jenna was so brave and strong. She told me her seatbelt had cut her neck and it was serious. I was able to move enough to hold her in my arms." A sob escaped from his lips. He gently touched his nose, right where it was broken. "Can you hand me a tissue?"

Hannah reached for the box. She needed one, too.

"Jenna knew she was dying. Made me promise to live enough for both of us. Told me just because I wouldn't be able to see her, that didn't mean she wouldn't be with me. Just before she died, she whispered, 'Always been a special bond between you and me, Scooter. And death won't break it. I'll always be with you'."

Hannah looked away when Dave's face momentarily flashed before her eyes. That last morning, he'd forgotten to kiss her before he drove off. *But he came back home just to embrace me and tell me how much he loved me.* An hour later, he was dead.

Sam was so wrapped up in his thoughts he didn't notice she'd looked away. "She died in my arms. It was almost a day and a half before they rescued me." He gripped her arms tightly. "I lost my mind, Hannah. I know you won't believe this, but during those lonely days, Jenna's spirit was with me. Assured me God told her He was sending someone very special to take her place as my best friend."

Sam grabbed her shoulders, bright eyes boring a path to her heart. "And she was right. That someone He sent... it was you."

It was suddenly hard to breathe as his words sank in, despite hearing the same thing before from both Sam's mother and sister. *Did You really bring me into Sam's life for this?* She couldn't help herself. She swept him in her arms, her cheek warmly against his.

Sam pushed her away. His eyes were full of something. *Fear?*

He was shaking so badly. "Hannah, I'm scared. I love you so much... and want you, but there are so many challenges before us. This whole age thing—I mean, I'm only six years older than your daughter. I know I'm still immature. Look how my selfishness hurt you last night. You deserve someone better than me. I don't see how we could make this work."

It's in my hands, now. This was the make or break moment. *Do I have the strength to really go through with it?* It was as if she was at the top of the room, watching both of them. Her eyes gravitated to Sam. So young, so strong, yet vulnerable. Before her eyes, they both aged to the vision she'd had that day she'd been hurt the first time. *What will my life be like with him... or without him?* Her heart answered for her. She leapt forward.

Hannah kissed his fingers. "It won't be easy, but I think we can do anything, if we give it our all..."

She had to laugh at his look of confusion. "What's that mean?"

"That means, if we try as hard as we can, we will make it work. No, not just work. This is going to be something very special, I feel it. And don't forget, God brought us together. " She held him tightly. "I think Jenna was right. God sent me for you, but He also sent you for me. To be *my* best friend, too. To teach me how to trust someone else, totally." Sam pulled away and stared at her. There was amazement in both of their eyes as they sat there.

You just changed my life, God. An hour ago, she'd been heartbroken, facing a future without Sam. Then Dale's brother appeared and she'd feared for her life. Now, she was free from the horror of the past. She had the means to provide for her family beyond her wildest dreams. And the love of her life was here in front of her. And he was in love with her. *Thank You for blessing me so richly.*

She smiled as she held his head in her hands. "You feel it, too. Beyond any explanation, here we are. You came to me. And I didn't realize it, but I've been here all along, waiting. Don't you want to kiss me?"

Sam's mouth fell open. Hannah couldn't wait any longer, she reached forward until her lips met his. *Rapture.* Never had she imagined a kiss could be so sweet. He finally pulled away to catch his breath.

Her chest tingled as she pulled him toward her again. "I've waited forever to do this. I love you, Samuel Espenshade." Their lips met and Hannah lost track of where she ended and Sam began. *This is Heaven.*

Chapter 27

J ake dropped his bags inside the door before kicking off his shoes. It felt good to be home after weeks on the road. He hadn't made it to a chair when the knock on the door drew his attention. He looked through the glass, quickly recognizing the attractive woman on the other side.

He threw open the door. "Jacob Elliot, how have you been?" she asked and wrapped him in a tight hug.

Jake felt the brush of her lips on his cheek, then he pulled back and took in the smiling face of his friend.

"Great to see you, Amy. I just got back from Panama."

"I know. The office seems awful lonely without you around to cause trouble. Did you enjoy the canal zone?"

Once again, he could detect the alcohol on her breath. *Poor woman, she's still mourning the loss of her husband.* "Not really. Kind of missed the snow and the traffic and the congestion that is New England."

"Miss anything else?"

"Yep." *Daisy.* "Nothing changed. Before I left, I found out she cancelled her cell phone, changed her e-mail address and quit her job. In my spare moments down there, between killing mosquitoes and standing in front of an air conditioner, I searched for her on the internet."

"And did you have any luck?"

He shook his head. "No. She seems to have fallen off the face of the earth. Maybe I should just give up."

Something about Amy's smile raised his interest. "You know, there are other options to find someone. Relatively low-tech options."

"Such as?"

Amy laughed out loud. "Snail mail, but I can't take the credit for this. I just happened to be walking past your desk the other day when I saw this." She held up an envelope. While it looked rather plain, he quickly recognized the handwriting on the address.

His mouth dropped open. "How did you know?"

"In today's modern world of commerce, few business letters are hand addressed." Her face sobered. "Maybe it's nothing, but then maybe it's everything. A voice in my head told me to get it to you as soon as possible. I hope I wasn't too pretentious in bringing it over."

Jake grabbed the letter, breathing in the aroma—Daisy's scent, Hyacinths. *Please tell me where you are.* He tore the envelope apart.

Dearest Jake,

Once again, I'd like to say I'm sorry for the way everything went down. I feel bad you believed I was playing you for a fool. Nothing was further from the truth.

I really wanted to be the one to tell you I was in love with you and that you were Mr. Right. You were then and still are. Nothing will ever change that.

I know it's too late for us and that you'll never forgive me, but I need you to understand one thing. From the moment I first saw you eighteen years ago, I loved you. I still do and eighteen years from now, I will love you even more.

It became too hard to stay here in Lancaster, so I'm moving to Hilo, Hawaii. My new cell number, e-mail address and home address are listed below. My biggest wish is that someday I'll open my door and you'll be standing there,

Also, my mom is throwing a surprise farewell party for me at the Essence of Tuscany Tea Room. If you want to say goodbye, please stop in. Date and time are below.

Know this last thing. I will love only you until the day I die.

Yours only, yesterday, today and forevermore,

Daisy Good

He released the page and it fluttered slowly to the floor.

Jake turned to see Amy studying his face. "You okay?"

He swallowed hard. "What time is it?"

"Noon. Something wrong?"

"I need a favor. Can you drop me off at Logan airport? We need to hurry. There still might be time."

Amy's smile was huge. "Do you need to grab some of this luggage?"

Jake held his hand over his heart. "Everything I need is already packed, right here."

***

"Surprise!" Daisy walked ahead of her mother into the Tea Room. Daisy had known about the party for some time. Vivian couldn't keep a secret if her life depended on it.

Almost everyone she'd worked with was gathered together to say goodbye. A woman Daisy had never met was in charge of the festivities for the Tea Room. Daisy knew the owner, Sophie, was out on maternity leave. Her favorite hostess, Ashley Snyder, had moved away after her fiancée, Harry Campbell, broke off the engagement. *It seems Ash and I have a lot in common. We both lost the loves of their lives.* And both were leaving the area to get away from the memories.

While the tea was fun, Daisy was having a hard time saying bye to her friends. In her role as office manager, she'd made it a point to get to know everyone, often creating great relationships. And it was hard to end them. Oh, they'd said they would keep in touch, but she knew she'd never hear from most of them again.

Joe Rohrer walked over, with a pretty woman Daisy had never met holding his hand. "Daisy, I'd like you to meet my girlfriend, Tara Miller. Tara is a nurse practitioner from my old practice. Tara, this is Daisy." Joe hung around after his girlfriend excused herself to use the restroom. He searched Daisy's eyes. "Any progress with Jake?"

Daisy shook her head. "No."

Joe patted her hand. "I don't know how you do it. You were so in love with him."

Daisy's eyes were scratchy. "I still am, but when you love someone, sometimes you have to let them go. If he comes back, it's love. If not, it was something else that was never meant to be." She engaged Joe's eyes. "Only time will tell." Daisy hugged him. "I'm going to miss you."

"I'll miss you, too. Best wishes and let me know how it works out. And if you ever need anything..." He pressed his lips to her forehead before leaving.

The bell on the door jingled. Daisy turned to see who'd entered, but the face of a familiar friend caught her eye. Trenton stood before her. "Hi, Daze. Hope you're not mad I came. Missed our friendship."

Daisy wrapped her arms around Trenton. "I missed it, too."

He released her and took her hands. "Sorry my big mouth ruined everything for you. Have you heard from him?"

Daisy forced a smile. "No. But hope springs eternal. One of these days, I'll turn around and he'll be there. I just know it."

Trenton's mouth dropped open and his eyes widened. He freed her hands and took a step backwards. She grew concerned. "Are you all right? Looks like you've seen a ghost."

His face was pale. Daisy realized the entire building had grown silent, quiet enough to hear a pin drop. And every eye was focused on something behind her. She caught a glimpse of the tears running down her mother's face. Daisy turned to see what everyone was looking at.

Her own eyes grew large when she caught sight of the man. He was three feet away, but on his knee. Daisy's hand flew to cover her mouth. "Is this a dream? Why are you here?"

The brilliance of Jake's eyes was almost blinding. "I came back, to beg your forgiveness. Realized I'd thrown away the most precious gift I'd ever received—your love. I'm hoping you'll not only forgive me, but say yes to my question. Will you marry me, Daisy?"

Her lips opened, but no words escaped. Daisy nodded, not knowing what to do with her hands. They were trembling as she reached for his face. Like a wave rushing to shore, Jake stood, wrapped her in his arms and lifted her off the floor. He kissed her, time and again. Sweet music surrounded her, as did the sound of people clapping and laughing. And she could feel his love wrap around her heart, her soul.

Jake pulled his lips from hers and gazed into her eyes. "I love you, Daisy. I was just too thickheaded to tell you before."

She placed her finger over his lips. "I was the one who was wrong. I should have told you that you were Mr. Right on the day we reconnected."

Jake kissed her again and then slipped his college ring on her finger. "This will have to do until we pick out a real engagement ring." He kissed her hand. "I knew you were the one that first day in the office. Wish I would've told you then. When did you first realize it?"

Daisy couldn't help but smile. "When I was thirteen, about seven seconds after we were introduced."

He brushed the hair from her eyes. "Maybe we should change our names. Just think, Daisy and Jake Right."

"No, thanks. I prefer Daisy Elliot. After all, that's been my lifelong dream. Kiss me again, so I know this isn't just a dream."

Jake's lips met hers and all at once she knew it wasn't just a fantasy. She really was in paradise.

Epilogue

H annah put the finishing touches on both wedding cakes. Her former employers, the Campbells, had become one of the first customers of her business—Hannah's Bakery. Her heart was filled with pride to be making the bridal cakes for her old boss, Harry, and for his brother, Edmund.

She felt eyes on her and turned to find Sam watching, his crooked smile shining her way. When Sam caught her eye, he laughed.

"What's so funny, Mr. Espenshade?"

"You are. No matter what you do, you can't help it, can you?"

She turned and giggled, knowing what was coming next. "Can't help what, Samuel?" she teased.

Her eyes closed in anticipation of his touch. She heard him shuffle across the floor and wrap his arms around her. Sam's voice was barely a whisper. "Being the most amazingly perfect woman in the world." His lips found the hollow of her neck and Sam worked his magic.

"Honey, we're working. Stop this. We might get caught."

He continued to kiss her, finding his way to her earlobe. "It's fine. I'll get away with it. I'm really tight with the boss."

The jingle of the bell on the front door stopped them in their tracks. She turned to Sam. "Why don't you get the keys and bring around the van. Then we'll load up the cakes together. Meanwhile, I'll take care of our customer."

Hannah's blood ran cold when she walked through the swinging doors separating the kitchen from the display area. A man was sticking his fingers in the layer cake she had on display. He grabbed a handful and took a bite. Two other men were doing the same to other display items.

After Kyle Parker licked the icing off his fingers, he threw the remainder on the floor before wiping his hands on his pants. He nodded toward the kitchen. "Those cakes back there. They're for the Campbell wedding, ain't they? For big fat Henry and that slime ball Edmund."

Hannah didn't know what to do, but she was scared. *Please keep Sam safe*. She refused to answer Kyle.

He laughed and nodded to the other two. "Smash those stupid cakes to smithereens while me and Hannah get reacquainted."

Hannah moved to block the men, but Kyle shoved her to the floor. "Payback's a bitch, ain't it?" He laughed. His two friends pushed the swinging doors open.

There were four loud thuds from the kitchen. Kyle laughed louder. "Wreck the joint, boys. Go ahead and..." The jerk's mouth dropped open. "What the hell?"

Sam walked through the door, holding his cane like a baseball bat. "Look who it is. Still a scumbag, huh, Kyle? Have to pick on a woman? Bully. If you think you're so tough, come at me. Or aren't you man enough?"

Kyle took a step toward him. "You're such a loser, Espenshade. Afraid I'll kick your ass again? That why you gotta use a cane?"

Hannah couldn't help but notice the fire in Sam's eyes. "Thanks to you, I'll walk with a cane the rest of my life. It's part of me, now." Sam laughed. "Like another arm." His eyes narrowed. "You owe the lady for the cake you defiled. Pay up now and *maybe* I won't press charges."

Kyle laughed again. "Make me." He started to move toward Sam.

Sam raised his cane as if he were standing in the batter's box. "Gladly."

No, no, no! The memory of the last fight between the two made Hannah sick. Kyle wouldn't fight fair and would end up hurting Sam, or worse. *Please send a miracle!* The door suddenly flew open and two police officers ran in. "Drop that stick."

Hannah's heart skipped a beat. Luckily, Sam immediately did as he was told.

"What's going on here?" the officer demanded.

Sam answered quickly. "I was just defending my wife. Glad you got here so quickly. I'm the one who called it in, officer." He pointed to the corner. "We've got it all on CCTV."

Hannah was shaking when Sam wrapped his arms around her. After the officers reviewed the video, they cuffed Kyle and his lowlife friends, read them their Miranda rights, and escorted them out the door. Her heartbeat slowly returned to double digits. Sam's lips were warm against her ear as he whispered, "Don't be scared. It's okay, honey. As long as I breathe, no one will ever make you feel that way again. I promise." *The same words you said to me in my dream.* He softly kissed her. "I love you, Hannah, always have, and I always will."

***

The usher seated Riley on the side of the aisle for the two brides' families and friends. The scent of gladiolas filled the air. While she hadn't been as close to Ashley Snyder as Jenna or Sam had been, she did know her. Because she'd only been an acquaintance, the invitation had been a surprise. *Speaking of surprises...*

She looked down the aisle and saw the usher take Hannah's arm. A second groomsman escorted Beth. The first usher called out, as he'd done for every guest. "Ladies and gentlemen, I'd like to introduce Mrs. Hannah Espenshade and her lovely daughter Beth. Also, Mister Samuel Espenshade and his daughter, Missi." Riley's heart was full of happiness for her brother's bliss.

Hannah entered the row and gave Riley a hug. Sam's wife sat on Riley's right. Beth also hugged her new aunt and took the chair to Riley's left. Sam sat next to his bride, but leaned forward and whispered, "You clean up good, sis." How he loved to tease her.

Something pulled at her dress. A tiny hand. "Me too. I wanna sit on Aunt Riley's lap." Riley gazed into the eyes of the five year old. *Hope I have a daughter like you, someday. But I need to find a man first.* The girl reached for Riley and deposited a wet, sloppy kiss on her aunt's lips.

"Of course, you can sit with me." She turned to her brother and his wife. "I understand the two of you had an exciting day. Mom told me how you got the best of Kyle."

Sam was smiling. The two men had been enemies since Sam took Kyle's spot as the starting catcher in little league. But Kyle always got the best of her brother when they got into fights. Until today. "The police arrested him. Henry Campbell's suggestion about installing the video system paid off. Maybe Kyle will finally leave us alone."

Riley could see the admiration in Hannah's eyes. "He's my hero, you know."

Riley glanced at the girl sitting on her lap. "I believe he's someone else's hero, too." Hannah nodded. "And the cakes made it here safely?"

Sam lifted an eyebrow. "Of course. Are you surprised?"

"No, but speaking of surprises, I've got one for you."

Hannah's smile grew. "Yeah? What is it? Don't keep us in suspense!"

Riley could hardly contain herself. She engaged Sam's eyes. "Remember the local television station where I interned in college?"

Sam's mouth dropped open. "The one here in Lancaster?"

"Yep. They have an opening for a sports reporter and guess what? The station manager personally called to let me know."

Sam reached across Hannah to squeeze Riley's hand tightly. "Does that mean you'll be moving home?"

Riley shrugged, but before she could answer, the usher called out another name. "Ladies and gentlemen, I'd like to introduce Mister Mickey Campeau." Almost every head turned to gawk at the giant.

Riley's head also turned. *The hockey player? Why would he be he*re?

Sam whispered, "That man is Ashley's friend. He rescued her when a gang was mugging her. They're pretty close."

Riley realized her mouth was hanging open and forced herself to shut it. *That would make a great human interest story*. The tall man suddenly glanced in her direction. It was as if time stopped. If the heat on her face was an indication, her face must be as red as her lipstick.

The usher paused three rows back, but Mickey pointed at Riley. "If you don't mind, I'd like to sit up there." The usher shrugged and Campeau took one stride before entering her row. It was comical the way Sam and Hannah had to lean way back in their seats to allow his passage.

Riley's eyes followed him until he stood before her.

His conversation was directed to Beth, but his eyes were on Riley. "Mind moving over, young miss?"

Beth's eyes were as big as dinner plates. "Uh, okay."

Riley was having trouble breathing. *Because he's a big star? Or is it the way he's looking at me?*

He sat next to Riley and extended his hand. "I'm Mickey Campeau and I know who you are."

Riley swallowed hard. "You do?" *How could he know me?*

"Yep. Don't know your full name, but seen you on TV a couple of times. You're that pretty sports girl from the Cleveland station, eh? Riley somethin' or other, yes?"

"E-E-Espenshade. Y-you've seen me? And remembered my name?"

"Aye. Never forget a face as pretty as yours."

If her face was hot before, it must be on fire now. "T-thank you, Mr. Campeau. It's a pleasure to meet you."

His laugh was like thunder, but Riley noticed his hands were shaking a little. *Not as bad as mine.* "Not Mister, not to you. Prefer you call me Mick. And it's a meeting to pleasure you."

Everyone around them must have been eavesdropping because the whole section broke out in laughter. The giant's face turned bright red. "I, uh, meant... it's like, uh, really nice to meet you." He leaned in close so he could whisper. "You're so much prettier in person than on the tube." His face was losing its color, turning pink. He smiled, revealing the gap between his canines.

For once in her life, Riley was speechless.

Little Missi broke the silence. "You're missing your tooths, like me. Did the tooth fairy give you money for them?" Missi smiled and she, too, was missing her front teeth.

Mickey reached down and touched the little girl's nose. "Nope. Keep mine in my pocket."

When he pulled his dental plate from his pocket and inserted it, Missi wrinkled her nose. "That's gross."

Riley couldn't help it. She roared with laughter. Mick did, too.

At that moment, the music started and the grooms began their descent down the aisle. Mickey leaned over to whisper in her ear. "Can only stay for the ceremony, but I'd like to see you sometime, if you don't mind. I'll give you my number and you give me yours, eh?"

She nodded. "I'd like that."

He winked. "Me, too."

After the exchange, Riley leaned back and caught the sly look on her sister-in-law's face. Hannah leaned toward her. "Hmm. First Sam and I, then the double wedding today... and after what I just witnessed? Looks like love is in the air."

Again, Riley knew her face was red. "I don't know what you're talking about."

Hannah reached over and grasped her hand. "Sure. Keep telling yourself that."

Riley stole another glance at Mick. He was looking at her and smiled. *Can life get any better than this?* Only time would tell.

***

Daisy stepped out onto the lanai. The trade winds were teasing her nose, laden with the scent of the islands, of rain and flowers.

"Hey, beautiful." She turned to the man of her dreams, her Mr. Right, now her husband. "On this morning's menu, we have mochas, guava pastries, fresh pineapple and the Hawaiian specialty, fried Spam."

Her heart leapt as he held her close, rubbing his nose against hers. "Why, Mr. Right, there's something I crave even more than food. Do you know me well enough to tell me what that is?"

His eyes shone brightly as he tilted his head. "Would it be this?" His lips were warm and soft.

Daisy's hands found their way to his hair, softly caressing him. "You know me very well, Mr. Right."

He kissed her again before leading her to the table. The mug was warm and the scent of chocolate permeated to her soul. *Life's just perfect. Thank you, Lord.*

Jake sighed as he gazed at her. "Guess we better decide."

She teased him as she ate. "I need my energy, so I vote for breakfast first."

He laughed and the corners of his eyes crinkled. "I was talking about where we'll live. The way I see it, we can stay here on the island, move to New England or head back to Pennsylvania."

Her fingernails teased the palm of the hand he offered. "We can live at the North Pole for all I care. As long as we're together."

"I feel the same way, but I do have one regret."

The look on his face disturbed her. "And what's that?"

"That I didn't notice how wonderful you were the first time I met you, when you were thirteen. I should have waited for you all those years, like you did for me."

Daisy's entire body relaxed. "We're together now and that's all that matters. So, where do you want to live?"

"Anywhere, as long as it's with you."

"No seriously. Where should we make our home?"

Jake rubbed his chin. "The islands are tempting, with the ocean and beauty that surrounds us. New England is gorgeous, but if I keep my job there, I'll be on the road all the time. My vote is we make our home in Lancaster, close to your... I mean, *our* family."

Daisy's heart pounded. "That's my choice, too. As soon as the honeymoon's over, let's go house hunting. I always loved the Paradise area. And, by the way, you read my mind... perfectly."

"As Mr. Right should."

She winked at him. "I don't want you to be Mr. Right anymore."

His eyes opened wide. "Why not?"

"Because, you know..."

The width of his smile was so beautiful. "Because of what's off limits?"

You read my mind. She nodded and popped some pineapple in her mouth. "I've got enough energy for a while. Ready for the main course?"

Jake swept her in his arms and headed toward the cottage. "If that's what my bride wants..." He rubbed his nose to hers and then kissed her deeply. "Know this one thing, Daisy Elliot. It doesn't matter where we live. Anywhere you are, that's where paradise is to me." He closed the door behind them.

The End

Get exclusive

never-before-published content!

www.chaswilliamson.com

A Paradise Short Story

Download your free copy of
Skating in Paradise today!

Other Books by this Author

Seeking Forever (Book 1)

Kaitlin Jenkins long ago gave up the notion of ever finding true love, let alone a soulmate. Jeremy is trying to get his life back on track after a bitter divorce and an earlier than planned departure from the military. They have nothing in common, except their distrust of the opposite sex.

An unexpected turn of events sends these two strangers together on a cross-country journey—a trip fraught with loneliness and unexpected danger. And on this strange voyage, they're forced to rely on each other—if they want to survive. But after the past, is it even possible to trust anyone again?

Seeking Forever is the first book of Chas Williamson's Seeking series, the saga of the Jenkins family over three generations.

Will Kaitlin and Jeremy ever be the same after this treacherous journey?

Seeking Happiness (Book 2)

Kelly was floored when her husband of ten years announced he was leaving her for another woman. But she isn't ready to be an old maid. And she soon discovers there's no shortage of men waiting in line.

Every man has his flaws, but sometimes the most glaring ones are well hidden. And now and then, those faults can force other people to the very edge, to become everything they're not. And when that happens to her, there's only one thing that can save Kelly.

Seeking Happiness is the second book of Chas Williamson's Seeking series, the saga of the Jenkins family over three generations.

Ride along with Kelly on one of the wildest adventures you can imagine.

Seeking Eternity (Book 3)
At eighteen, Nora Thomas fell in love with her soulmate and best friend, Stan Jenkins. But Nora was already engaged to a wonderful man, so reluctantly, Nora told Stan they could only be friends. Stan completely disappeared (well, almost), from her world, from her life, from everywhere but Nora's broken heart.

Ten painful years later, the widow and mother of two was waiting tables when she looked up and found Stan sitting in her section. But she was wearing an engagement ring and Stan, a wedding ring. Can a woman survive when her heart is ripped out a second time?

Seeking Eternity is the third book of Chas Williamson's Seeking series, a glimpse at the beginning of the Jenkins' family saga through three generations.

Will Nora overcome all odds to find eternal happiness?

Seeking the Pearl (Book 4)
Eleanor Lucia has lived a sad and somber life, until she travels to London to open a hotel for her Aunt Kaitlin. For that's where Ellie meets Scotsman Henry Campbell and finally discovers true happiness. All that changes when Ellie disappears without a trace and everyone believes she is dead, well almost everyone.

But Henry and Ellie have a special bond, one that defies explanation. As if she were whispering in his ear, Henry can sense Eleanor begging him to save her. And Henry vows he will search for her, he will find her and he will rescue her, or spend his last breath trying.

Seeking the Pearl is the exciting finale of Chas Williamson's Seeking series, the culmination of the three generation Jenkins' family saga.

Henry frantically races against time to rescue Ellie, but will he be too late?

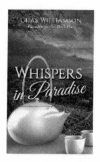

Whispers in Paradise (Book 1)

Ashley Campbell never expected to find love, not after what cancer has done to her body. Until Harry Campbell courts her in a fairy tale romance that exceeds even her wildest dreams. But all that changes in an instant when Harry's youngest brother steals a kiss, and Harry walks in on it.

Just when all her hopes and dreams are within reach, Ashley's world crumbles. Life is too painful to remain in Paradise because Harry's memory taunts her constantly. Yet for a woman who has beaten the odds, defeating cancer not once, but twice, can anything stand in the way of her dreams?

Whispers in Paradise is the first book in Chas Williamson's Paradise series, stories based loosely around the loves and lives of the patrons of Sophie Miller's Essence of Tuscany Tea Room.

Which brother will Ashley choose?

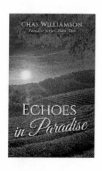

Echoes in Paradise (Book 2)

Hannah Rutledge rips her daughters from their Oklahoma home in the middle of the night to escape a predator from her youth. After months of secrecy and frequent moves to hide her trail, she settles in Paradise and ends up working with Sam Espenshade, twelve years her junior. Sam wins her daughters' hearts, and earns her friendship, but because of her past, can she ever totally trust anyone again?

Yet, for the first time since the death of her husband, Hannah's life is starting to feel normal, and happy, very happy. But a violent attack leaves Sam physically scarred and drives a deep wedge between them. To help heal the wounds, Hannah is forced from her comfort zone and possibly exposes the trail she's tried so hard to cover.

Echoes in Paradise is the second book in Chas Williamson's Paradise series, an exciting love story with Sophie Miller's Essence of Tuscany Tea Room in background.

When the villain's brother shows up on Hannah's doorstep at midnight on Christmas Eve, were the efforts since she left Oklahoma in vain?

Courage in Paradise (Book 3)

Sportscaster Riley Espenshade returns to southcentral Pennsylvania so she can be close to her family while growing her career. One thing Riley didn't anticipate was falling for hockey's greatest superstar, Mickey Campeau, a rough and tall Canadian who always gets what he wants... and that happens to be Riley. Total bliss seems to be at her fingertips, until she discovers Mickey also loves another girl.

The 'other girl' happens to be Molly, a two-year old orphan suffering from a very rare childhood cancer. Meanwhile, Riley's shining career is rising to its zenith when a new sports network interviews her to be the lead anchor. Just when her dream job falls into her lap, Mickey springs his plan on her, a quick marriage, adopting Molly and setting up house.

Courage in Paradise is Chas Williamson's third book in the Paradise series, chronicling the loves and lives of those who frequent Sophie Miller's Essence of Tuscany Tea Room.

Riley is forced to make a decision, but which one will she choose?

Stranded in Paradise (Book 4)

When Aubrey Stettinger is attacked on a train, a tall, handsome stranger comes to her assistance, but disappears just as quickly. Four months later, Aubrey finds herself recuperating in Paradise at the home of a friend of a friend.

When she realizes the host's brother is the hero from the train, she suspects their reunion is more than a coincidence. Slowly, and for the first time in her life, Aubrey begins to trust—in family, in God and in a man. But just when she's ready to let her guard down, life once again reminds her she can't trust anyone. Caught between two worlds, Aubrey must choose between chasing her fleeting dreams and carving out a new life in this strange place.

Stranded in Paradise is the fourth book in the Paradise series, chronicling the loves and lives of those who frequent Sophie Miller's Essence of Tuscany Tea Room.

Will Aubrey remain *Stranded in Paradise*?

Christmas in Paradise (Book 5)

True love never dies, except when it abandons you at the altar.

Rachel Domitar has found the man of her dreams. The church is filled with friends and family, her hair and dress are perfect, and the honeymoon beckons, but one knock at the door is about to change everything.

Leslie Lapp's life is idyllic – she owns her own business and home, and has many friends – but no one special to share her life... until one dark and stormy afternoon when she's forced off the highway. Will the knock at her door be life changing as well?

When love comes knocking at Christmas, will they have the courage to open the door to paradise?

About the Author

Chas Williamson's lifelong dream was to write. He started writing his first book at age eight, but quit after two paragraphs. Yet some dreams never fade...

It's said one should write what one knows best. That left two choices—the world of environmental health and safety... or romance. Chas and his bride have built a fairytale life of love. At her encouragement, he began writing romance. The characters you'll meet in his books are very real to him, and he hopes they'll become just as real to you.

True Love Lasts Forever!

Follow Chas on
www.bookbub.com/authors/chas-williamson

Enjoyed this book?
Please consider placing a review on Amazon!

Made in the USA
Middletown, DE
21 August 2021